Nugget, Coins, and Murder

A Cozy Magic Midlife Mystery

Silver Circle Cat Rescue Mysteries
Book 3

Leanne Leeds

Nugget, Coins, and Murder
Silver Circle Cat Rescue Mysteries #3
ISBN: 978-1-950505-90-6

Published by Badchen Publishing
14125 W State Highway 29
Suite B-203 119
Liberty Hill, TX 78642 USA

Cats know how to obtain food without labor, shelter without confinement, and love without penalties.

W.L. George

Contents

Chapter One

The August sun beat down on the crowd gathered at Lions Park, sending rivulets of sweat trickling down the back of my neck. I fanned myself vigorously with the fundraising flyer, trying to avoid becoming a human sprinkler system as Landon and I made our way over to one of the picnic tables. It was, mercifully, set up under the shade of a sprawling live oak.

"It's hot enough to boil copper out in this inferno," Landon said, wiping his brow. "I'd say this calls for a cold beer."

"You think anything calls for a cold beer."

"You're not wrong."

"Iced tea for me," I said.

He dipped his chin in a cordial nod, a smile playing about his mouth as he headed toward the coolers set up along the side of the picnic area.

As he walked away, I watched him go for a second. Then I looked around the jam-packed park, full of people enjoying the sunny day. In the distance, I spotted a familiar acquaintance in a bright purple sun hat, waving excitedly when she saw me. "Eleanor! Wait there, I'm coming!"

"Hi, Blanche," I said and waved.

Blanche Goldfinch, her usual prim and proper self, carefully picked her way across the grass in low heels and joined me at the table. "Eleanor, love, this heat is unbearable, don't you think? Who in their right mind would expect a turnout with the mercury this high? But turn out they did. It seems free beer trumps heat stroke every time!" She fanned herself furiously with a brochure, her frown deepening at the sight of my mid-sleeve shirt and slacks. "Well, don't you look positively casual. Aren't you melting?"

I laughed. "It comes with living in Texas, I'm afraid. At least Waldo was smart enough to do a barbecue fundraiser and have lots of cold drinks on hand. Including the beer." The aroma of smoked brisket wafted through the air as if on cue. My stomach rumbled. "Poor man must be melting at that pit over there. How's he looking in the polls against Mayor Winthrop so far?"

"Waldo didn't come up with the free beer idea. That was all me." Blanche sighed. "If by polls you mean comments and followers on SocialBook, not as well as we'd hope. That horrid woman always manages to squirm her way out of any controversy, and you just know she'll stoop to any level to win." She shook her head, lips pursed. "After that nonsense she pulled with the Tablerock Cottages, I sincerely hope she doesn't resort to more 'dirty tricks' against poor Waldo. He's trying so hard, the dear."

The Tablerock Cottages Museum situation still made my blood boil.

A few months ago, Mayor Winthrop proposed turning the historic cottages Blanche's great-great-grandfather built into luxury condos by selling the town-owned land to an out-of-town developer, steamrolling opposition from concerned citizens and ignoring the tourism.

It was clearly just a greedy ploy for cash and clout, and it was no surprise to me that Mayor Jessa appeared willing to destroy everything charming and unique about Tablerock to line her pockets. Luckily, at the final hour, Blanche sued, claiming the town's sale of the land went against her family's stipulations when they donated it.

The local magistrate ruled in favor of Blanche, furnishing Mayor Jessa Winthrop with one more adversary to add to her tally.

"If that museum situation didn't make people see who she is, I don't know what will," I told Blanche.

The crunch of footsteps on grass heralded Landon's return. He handed me my red plastic cup of sweet tea (and gave one to Blanche, the dear man) before settling on the picnic table bench beside me. "Here's hoping she keeps showing who she is so people will vote her out," he said, twisting the cap off his beer.

"From your mouth, Landon," Blanche said. She held up the tea. "Thank you."

"I know Waldo's got a fighting chance. She's not as popular as she thinks, especially after the situation with her son and the museum." He raised the amber-colored bottle in a toast, the glass glinting in the sunlight. "To a fair election and a new mayor!"

Blanche and I clinked our cups against his. "Hear, hear!"

The odds might be stacked against Waldo, but if anyone could give our unscrupulous mayor a run for her money, it was Tablerock's own martial arts master. Mayor Winthrop didn't stand a chance against his grass-roots support and good old-fashioned Texas charm.

Well, I hoped, anyway.

Blanche glanced at her phone and sighed, annoyance flickering across her features. "Where is that man? He promised he'd be here by now." She shook her head. "I swear, sometimes I think Harold has no interest in what happens to this town. He's always off doing heaven knows what." She slipped her phone back into her pocket. "I don't understand how coins can fascinate someone so much."

"How's business been lately?" Landon asked.

Blanche brushed his question off with a flick of her wrist. "Booming as always. But what good is success if you never slow down enough to enjoy it?" She frowned.

"I swear, Landon, I'd trade every penny of any age for a single undivided hour of that man's time and attention." Her words took on a hushed quality. "Thirty-five years of marriage, and it's like I barely exist some days."

Blanche's frank admission about her marriage caught me off guard, leaving me slightly uncomfortable. While Harold's workaholic tendencies were common knowledge, her tone hinted at deeper troubles beneath the veneer of their prosperous life.

"I'm sorry to hear that," I said.

And I was, though, if I really thought about it, Blanche's marital issue should be no surprise. Harold Goldfinch poured himself into the rare coin and bullion business he'd built from the ground up, and his obsession with growing the company often seemed to come at the expense of his wife's commitments.

Blanche managed a weak smile. "Yes, well, no need to fret over my troubles. What's done is done." She straightened, smoothing her skirt. "Now, what else can we do to help Waldo's campaign? I won't have that harpy of a mayor ruining this town with her greed and corruption one more year without putting up a fight. Especially now that someone's willing to run against her."

I couldn't agree more.

Rallying behind Waldo was one of the few ways we could defend Tablerock from Jessa Winthrop's self-serving ambitions. I felt a duty to back him as much as I could, too, seeing as how Fiona Blackwell had provided the funds for his bid at the town's highest office in her will.

The same will that gave me the Wardwell Mansion.

Now a cat rescue.

Landon launched into an animated stream of suggestions to sway undecided voters in the last few weeks of the campaign. I chimed in with ideas for letters to the editor, social media campaigns, and organizing meet-and-greets where Waldo could connect directly with constituents.

Blanche's expression shifted from optimism to genuine excitement as she tapped each new suggestion into the memo app on her phone, lavender nails clicking on the screen.

"A fundraising gala." Blanche's eyes widened at my suggestion, manicured hands freezing over the keyboard on her phone. "We host an elegant dinner, auction off some bigger ticket items from local businesses... it's the perfect opportunity to raise major donations and make a final push for exposure and votes. We can invite the local media and turn it into an event that helps Waldo's popularity spike at the right time."

"Perfect," I said as Blanche's fingers flew across the phone screen again, hat tipping with the fervor of her typing.

"We could even have it at the Manor!" she said, her eyes aglow. Then suspicion crept in, narrowing them. "You do keep those cats caged at times, I trust?"

"Nope, we're cage-free," I said, standing from the

creaky picnic table bench. I brushed away a few persistent and determined fire ants that had crawled onto the back of my bare calves. "No cages for kitties at my place. Sorry. There are lots of places you could have it, though. I'm happy to help. Just call me later."

I caught my boyfriend's glance and motioned toward Landon's truck.

I was ready for air conditioning.

A blessed wave of cool, conditioned air enveloped me. Even though it was laced with the scents of antiseptic and fishy kibble, I breathed it in like it was perfumed with roses. A cacophony of meows erupted as the rescue residents caught a glimpse of my arrival through the slats separating the café from the front door.

Before I could say hello, Evie looked up at me, her eyebrows knit with worry. "Mom, someone just abandoned this cat on our doorstep and sped off." A plump calico purred blissfully in her arms, soft black, white, and copper fur swelling with each rumbling purr.

"What do you mean? Someone just left her on the front porch?"

"Yep. She ran out of her car with the cat in her arms, dumped the cat on the porch, hopped back in her car, and drove away. I was watching through the window."

I looked down at the cat.

Calicos are not actually a cat breed. They're a color

pattern characterized by white, orange, and black fur splotches. The distinctive tricolor coat color pattern results from specific genes carried on the X chromosome. Because of that, calicos are almost always female.

I disliked that someone randomly dropped a cat on our doorstep, and I wondered if we needed to invest in a box for cats like the fire department's baby box. Wardwell Manor had a lot of land, but it was situated half a mile from a bustling highway—half a mile was nothing for a cat.

If people intended to abandon cats on our doorstep and counted on us to scoop them up before they strayed into danger...

I sighed.

People really annoyed me sometimes.

Landon came in and immediately complimented the new arrival's vibrant colors. "She looks a little like Sundae, that calico that always greets me." Suddenly, he frowned, squinting at the cat in my daughter's arms. "Actually, this cat looks an awful lot like the shop cat Harold keeps over at Goldfinch Coins. Plump, long-haired, and I'd swear it has the same fur pattern."

"Maybe his cat got out, and the woman was well-meaning in dropping her off here," I said, trying to put a Samaritan spin on the dangerous action. I looked at Evie. "Did you scan her for a chip? Laurie makes everyone get one, and the Goldfinches have lived here forever. If that is Harold's cat, she's probably Laurie's patient."

Evie shook her head. "Was just going to head over to Laurie's wing to check."

"Well, hold on. Let me just call Harold and see if his cat's lost," I said.

I looked up and tapped the number to call Goldfinch Coins, listening to it ring several times before the answering machine picked up with a curt message in Harold's gruff, no-nonsense voice about temporarily shortened summer hours.

"No answer. Go ahead to Laurie's and scan for that chip," I told Evie. "If this cat belongs to Harold, the microchip—if the cat has one—should clear things up quickly."

As Evie walked toward the mansion's east wing with the calico, Landon turned to me. "Maybe we should try calling Blanche instead. You have her number?"

"I do," I told him, scrolling through my contacts.

Luckily, our shared interest in Waldo's campaign for mayor led to an exchange of phone numbers at a local fundraiser (between hobnobbing with small town socialites and small business power players.) I put the call on speaker, and we listened to it ring several times before Blanche's voicemail picked up.

Landon extended his hand toward me.

"Blanche, it's Ellie. We found a cat that looks a lot like Harold's shop cat. Please give us a call back if your cat's lost so we can get her home." I disconnected, frowning. "You're sure it's Harold's cat?"

"Pretty sure," Landon said. "I was just in Goldfinch

Coins last week buying an uncirculated Morgan silver dollar for my dad's birthday in September. While I was there, that cat went crazy, hissing and swatting at Harold's lawyer, so I had reason to stare at it. Nearly took his eye out. Harold threw the guy out of the store."

I arched one brow skeptically. "The cat attacked Harold's own lawyer?"

"Yep. I've heard of dogs not liking people and getting aggressive, but I never heard of a cat doing it."

I sure had. "You must be blessed to socialize with incredibly nice people."

He flashed me a winsome smile. "Well, I do have great taste."

Before I could respond, Evie came back. "Mom, the cat's chip says her name is Nugget, and Landon was right. She belongs to Harold Goldfinch."

"Like I said, Evie, the cat probably just ran out of the store and got lost. We have so many tourists here on the weekends that they might not have known who the cat belonged to and just brought it here."

Even as I said it, a nagging feeling tugged at me.

Harold's shop was always open on Saturdays, yet no one picked up the phone. Moreover, the cat had never run out of the shop previously. Why today? An uneasy feeling settled in the pit of my stomach.

"Did you try calling Harold's cell phone?" Evie asked.

"I don't have it. I called the store and Blanche, but no answer."

A frown line creased Evie's forehead. "Should we just drive the cat back to Harold's shop? If we take Nugget in, we'll have to quarantine her for three days to check for any illnesses before introducing her to the other cats or releasing her back to them. Wouldn't it be easier on her and us if we just took her home?"

She had a point.

Local regulations said that if we processed a pet, we needed to quarantine it for three days before releasing it to anyone. An adopter, a claimed owner. Anyone. What the regulations conveniently failed to specify, however, was that we actually had to bring said animal into the system in the first place.

That, my friend, is what we call a loophole.

At its heart, Tablerock remained a tight-knit small town community, and doing good deeds for your neighbors was simply a way of life in the rolling Texas hills. Doing Harold a favor was just in our DNA.

"You're right. Let's bring back Nugget ourselves," I said. "Landon and I can run over there. It just takes a few minutes and the shop's right down the highway. Why don't you go grab me a carrier?"

If you're wondering why I didn't bring Nugget up to the isolation room so I could talk to her directly, it's a fair question.

We were able to establish pretty quickly that the

fluffy calico had a home, and we found where she belonged without using the magic talking drink platter thing. If we don't need to use it, we try not to. Despite its usefulness, I wasn't very relaxed about the platter's ability, and it was a secret I guarded carefully.

Well, that we guarded carefully. Because a few people knew.

Well, somewhat carefully.

Okay, I was trying to be better.

The wheels of Landon's truck crackled on the loose gray gravel of the shopping center parking lot. As we prowled the aisles of crammed spaces hunting for a vacant spot, a flare of red and blue caught my eye. Landon inhaled sharply at my side.

"The police are here. And an ambulance," he said.

"I know. I see them."

Two emergency vehicles were angled in at the far end of the lot, blocking the storefront of Goldfinch Coins. Their lights spun and flickered as a pair of officers stood before the entrance. Yellow police tape cordoned off the front of the building.

An ominous feeling settled into my stomach as we sat in loaded silence. "I hope Harold's all right," I said. I glanced at Nugget, sitting serenely in her carrier, buckled into the back seat. "The cat doesn't seem stressed or concerned—"

"Look, there's Mario."

Landon maneuvered into an empty space a few rows behind the emergency vehicles just as Officer Mario

Lopez broke away from his fellow officers and rushed toward us, boots thudding on the pavement. His usual easygoing smile was nowhere to be found.

"He doesn't look happy," I said.

Landon was quiet as he rolled down his window.

"No," Mario said, his face visible through the open car window. "Leave now. Go. Be on your way."

"Friendly greeting." Landon met my gaze, brow furrowed, and then turned back toward Mario. "What happened?" Landon asked as if Mario had not just ordered us gone.

"You really just don't listen, do you? What are you two even doing here?" Mario asked, glancing between us. "You need to leave. Now. I don't want to have to explain how the crazy cat lady and her carpenter boyfriend keep getting mixed up in Tablerock's deaths."

"Deaths?" Landon's frown deepened, forehead creasing. "Look, just tell us what's going on, Mario. We're here for a legitimate reason. We came to return Harold's cat, and now you've cordoned off his shop. You need to tell us what's happening."

His eyes darted between us while he grappled with this conundrum, seeming as indecisive as yours truly in an ice cream parlor. Finally, with a deep sigh, Mario said, "Look, I can't give you too many details right now. This might be an active crime scene." The cop grimaced. "It might not. But you both need to get out of here immediately."

My gaze wandered past Mario to the police tape and

strange, spinning lights beyond. "What do you mean, 'might be' a crime scene?" I asked.

Mario's lips pressed into a thin line. "I can't share details of an open investigation. As I've said before. Please, just go. I don't want you involved in this."

"I think you're the one not listening." Landon tapped the steering wheel, his jaw set and eyes flashing in annoyance. "As we mentioned, we're already involved, Mario. This"—Landon hitched his thumb toward the back seat—"is Harold's cat—someone dropped it off at Ellie's shelter this morning. It's confirmed. We're not guessing. Evie checked the microchip. Now tell us what happened here."

Mario's gaze dropped to the cat carrier in the back seat, his brow furrowing.

After a long moment, he sighed in resignation and practically stuck his head into the truck through the window, voice low. "Harold Goldfinch is dead," he said. "Appears he fell off a ladder in his shop and hit his head. The county coroner's on the way."

Chapter Two

The county coroner emerged from Goldfinch Coins, the bells tied to the front door jangling as it swung shut behind him. A black body bag lay atop the gurney.

A lumpy, lifeless form stretched beneath the zippered black body bag on the gurney he wheeled out. The rubber wheels squeaked an eerie tune as he advanced past detectives lingering under the Goldfinch Coins' neon "Open" sign, now a mockingly bright sentinel over the crime scene.

My heart sank at the sight.

Harold Goldfinch.

He really was gone.

I didn't know him very well. Harold had never quite... endeared himself to me. He'd always seemed like the kind of guy who didn't have a lighthearted bone in his body—cheerfulness and Harold? Not on speaking terms. I had enough dour people in my past. I avoided them like the plague.

Though... maybe I was being too harsh. Harold was tolerable in the way you find your moderately congenial neighbors tolerable. They were good at heart, even if their personality was somewhat grating.

At least, he seemed so.

Good at heart, that is.

Though if someone clocked him on the head, maybe he wasn't.

I watched as the coroner loaded the gurney into the back of the van, securing the body bag in place before slamming the doors shut.

Landon shook his head, eyes distant. "What an odd accident," he murmured, rubbing at his chin, fingernails rasping on the day's stubble. "Falling off a ladder in his own store. Such a mundane thing, and then—" He slammed a fist into his palm. "Boom, tragedy. Just out of nowhere."

The crowd swelled and pulsed around the ambulance like spectators at a morbid circus sideshow. As I scanned the parking lot, which held far more gawkers and gossiping locals than any medical emergency should rightly attract, an uneasy feeling prickled at my neck.

"Do you really buy that?" I asked Landon. "Harold was obsessed with that shop. I think he'd been here for over twenty years and up and down that ladder dozens of times a day; suddenly, now, he makes a mistake? That just doesn't sound right to me at all."

His gaze drifted to the window, brow furrowed as if in troubled thought. "You think the police have it wrong?" Landon's gaze searched my face.

"Well, maybe not. Maybe they have suspicions, and Mario just doesn't know. I don't know." I nodded toward a group of people clustered nearby, talking among themselves. A portly, balding man standing slightly apart from them kept looking over his shoulder at the shop, face pale. "You see that man over there, the nervous one who keeps glancing at the building? He was arguing with someone on the phone when we pulled in. Yelling, actually. Now he's acting all shifty."

Landon peered through the window like a sentry at his post. His gaze remained fixed on the man across the parking lot for a while, tracking his progress with a sharpness that belied his relaxed posture. "Maybe," he murmured.

"Maybe, nothing. The guy looks like he just robbed a bank."

We could both see he had furtive, nervous energy about him, constantly looking over his shoulder and pacing. His body language seemed off, somehow tense and agitated, and his hair shined like he'd dumped an entire bottle of product in it. "Yeah, okay, I'll give you that. He seems more upset than some random bystander would be. You think it's because he knows something about what happened?"

"Maybe. Or maybe I just have an overactive imagination." I sighed, watching as the emergency vehicles began to disperse, their work concluded. "But my gut says this was no accident. And Harold's cat showing up abandoned on our doorstep this morning?" I glanced in the back seat. "Too weird a coincidence."

"Your gut, huh?" He quirked an eyebrow at me, a smile playing at the corners of his mouth.

I shrugged. "My gut told me I should go out with you."

His smile broke free then, crinkling the corners of his eyes. "Did it now?"

"What can I say?" I tilted my head. "This gut has been honing its instincts for over fifty years. Gotten pretty sharp by now."

A sudden squeal of tires caught our attention.

As Landon and I watched, a sleek silver sedan came careening into the parking lot, rolling to an abrupt stop with a protesting squeal of brakes. The driver's side door flew open, and Mabel Berry, Harold's assistant from the coin shop, leaped out—without putting the vehicle into park.

It began slowly rolling forward, inching ahead and gathering speed on the slight decline of the lot. Mabel didn't seem to notice or care, oblivious to the potential disaster unfolding behind her. She stumbled toward the police in high-heeled shoes that threatened to pitch her face-first onto the asphalt with every step.

"Please, you have to tell me what happened!" Her hands clasped together in front of her lips, trembling, as she glanced between the officers in a panic. "Is Mr. Goldfinch all right?"

The sedan coasted by behind her, driverless, picking up speed. Finally, we heard metal crunching as it collided with Deputy Don Markham's police cruiser.

I could hear poor Don swear loudly, rushing over to assess the damage.

Mabel's voice rose to a hysterical pitch, tears spilling onto her cheeks. "He has to be okay! Please, somebody, tell me he's—"

The officer's face fell at her words. Whatever silent answer was written in that grim expression caused Mabel's pleas to abruptly transform into ragged, choking sobs that shook her thin shoulders with the force of her grief.

Mabel's anguished sobs carried to where we sat in the truck, audible above the crowd's din. As the vultures continued to gather near Landon's truck, they gawked at the scene unfolding. Within the first minute of Mabel's sobbing, they'd lowered their heads together to swap hushed speculations.

"I bet she did it. Probably pushed him off that ladder herself."

"Always thought there was something off about her. Creepy, the way she was so devoted to Goldfinch. Never dated. Not normal to be that involved with someone else's husband, I'll tell you what."

"In this town?" a woman asked wryly. "I thought

being involved with someone else's husband was almost a prerequisite!"

"Don't let Jessa hear you saying that. Your house might accidentally get condemned. You know, my cousin volunteers with Mabel at the thrift store. Said she had become obsessed and possessive over him."

The gossip grew louder.

One woman with a helmet of stiff blond curls raised a manicured hand to her lips, eyes gleaming with scandalized delight. "I heard they were having an affair. Bet she flew into a rage when he tried to end it."

"Shocking!" her redheaded friend crowed. "Simply scandalous!"

Talk buzzed and murmured through the crowd, thriving on two parts rumor and innuendo for every part truth. Each new theory was more absurd and unkind than the last.

Landon and I exchanged a troubled glance.

Though as distasteful as I found the gossip, I knew rumors about Mabel's unrequited feelings for her boss had circulated for years. I'd never thought about them much. Harold seemed devoted to Blanche—even with her complaints about his lack of attention, she never seemed to suspect he was unfaithful to her.

My certainty wavered as that crowd traded tales of Mabel's erratic behavior.

Was our killer standing in plain sight, mourning the man she'd murdered?

Or maybe we were just being nosy neighbors, seeing

things that weren't there, just like those gossiping biddies in the parking lot.

Landon and I rode back to the cat rescue gabbing back and forth on theories and possibilities surrounding the disturbing events at Goldfinch Coins. My mind raced with questions and suspicions—along with, I'll admit, a healthy dose of self-doubt.

Were we making mountains out of molehills?

Seeing intrigue and foul play where there were simply tragic accidents?

"You know Markham's going to show up here eventually," Landon said as we pulled in. "He'll want to know who dropped that cat off, and Mario will no doubt let him know that we have the cat. They'll probably also want to look at the shelter's security footage." He put his truck in park. "We may want to take a look before he does."

"If they think there's a murder, he might. But according to Mario, it doesn't seem like they think it's a murder."

Landon's hand found mine, his fingers lacing tight through my own. "You know, after the complete bungling the town's police did of Ben Tyson's murder, I can't help but wonder if the county decided the local police don't need to know all that much about their investigation," he said. "Personally? I'd wait to hear what

Markham had to say. I wouldn't put too much stock into what the local police supposedly know about this latest situation."

I had to admit the botching of Ben Tyson's murder case could have damaged the department's credibility and trust with the county officials. Tablerock had a criminal enterprise running under their nose and managed two searches of the criminal headquarters without finding anything—or even getting very curious about the steaming clues right in front of their noses.

And they were steaming.

Literally. One clue was steam.

Landon's theory that the county officials were elbowing in at the get-go to take over the investigation, keen to avoid another embarrassing display of police ineptitude, was plausible—as much as I hated to admit it.

With Nugget the cat peering out curiously from inside her carrier, I reached behind the seat and scratched at the wire mesh door. "You'll be okay, buddy, I promise," I told him. She butted her head against the door, pushing her whole body along with it in her enthusiasm. "Okay, we can get you out of there as soon as we bring you inside."

We hurried up the walkway and pushed in through the front door. Landon held it open as I maneuvered through, lugging the carrier gently as Nugget's inquisitive meows echoed from within, eager to explore new surroundings.

Before we closed the door behind us, Evie and Matt

were in the foyer. My daughter's eyes were wide and full of worry. "Mom, is it true about Harold Goldfinch?"

Matt put an arm around her shoulders. "My friend Mark called me from Silver Spoon. He said the whole shopping center's buzzing about it, claiming Harold Goldfinch died."

I handed Evie the cat carrier holding Nugget. The calico meowed plaintively from within, reminding us of her captive presence.

I sighed. "I'm afraid they're right. Well, your friend Mark is, at any rate. The coroner was there, and Harold Goldfinch is no longer with us, poor man."

At my words, Nugget let out an agitated hiss from inside the carrier, fur puffing up around her face in distress. Her ears flattened back, and she shrank away from the side of the cage.

In hushed tones, Landon and I recounted for the kids what we had each witnessed from our impromptu stakeout in the parking lot. Landon passed along the gossip and rumors buzzing through the crowd we'd endured next to us, grim tales that were met with grave expressions and worried frowns.

As our covert conversation ended, I couldn't help glancing up at the manor's second floor, gaze drawn toward the secluded and soundproofed isolation room at the end of the hall. The room which now housed Fiona's enchanted platter.

If anyone had real answers here, it might be Nugget.

I met Evie's gaze and tilted slightly toward the staircase, raising my eyebrows in silent question. She nodded almost imperceptibly.

Message received.

"Well, we should get Nugget settled in. Make sure she has food and water. A quiet place to relax." I brushed off my hands, keenly aware of Matt and Landon watching the exchange between Evie and me. "Evie, why don't you carry her to the isolation room?"

"Sure, Mom." Evie scooped up the carrier. "Come on, Nugget. We'll get you out of this thing and into something a little more comfy."

"Oh heavens no, I simply will not have it! You shan't be bringing that dreadful creature into my chambers! Is it a canine? If that bumbling fool of a veterinarian has sent another dog up to my room again, I shall give you such a tongue-lashing that you'll wish you'd never been born!" Belladonna huffed indignantly from her glowing perch atop the magical platter, sleek black fur puffed out until she resembled an outraged feather duster.

"Now, Bella—"

"Don't you 'now, Bella' me! You rabble seem to forget to whom this grand estate properly belongs! This has been the ancestral home of the Wardwells for generations!"

"Just a couple of them," I told her.

"The sheer audacity and impertinence you display

by even trodding upon the hallowed ground of this manor is insulting. Begone from my sight, posthaste, before my sharpened claws give you the thrashing you deserve! Uncultured swine!"

"Okay, let's start this over. Good morning, Belladonna!" I said in a cheerful sing-song voice, ignoring her furious speech.

Evie chimed in with an equally bright "Hello!"

"Top of the morning to you," Matt added.

Not to be outdone, Landon tipped an imaginary hat. "How do, Miss Belladonna? Having a good morning, are we?"

Our affectionate greeting only caused the temperature of Belladonna's temper to rise. She hissed venomously at our approach, hackles raised and eyes glowing angrily. "What is the meaning of this tomfoolery?! Why ever are you carrying on in this manner? Have you taken complete leave of your senses?"

"No meaning," I said. "Just a good day, and we're saying hello."

"How are you this fine morning?" Ellie added.

"It really is lovely to see you," Matt told the angry black cat.

On most days, Belladonna had a temper as dark as her fur, and our friendly salutations had stoked the coals of her ire for reasons known only to her. "Cease this nonsense at once! Your foolish pleasantries do not amuse me. I demand to know why you've disturbed my rest and what beast you've brought to torment me now." Her hair now raised like porcupine quills, Belladonna morphed from a feather duster to a miniature hellcat fit to spawn demons. "I can smell it."

"No beast, Belladonna, just a cat," I assured her. "We have questions for this cat." I pointed to the carrier. "Her name is Nugget, and we were hoping you would allow her to use your plate."

It was really my plate.

But with Belladonna, it was easier sometimes to let her think... well, whatever she wanted.

"Nugget?" Her ears had been pinned back, and her eyes burned with embers of anger, but Belladonna's indignation morphed into keen interest at the mention of another cat. Ears up, fur down, eyes rounding, she peered over the edge of the platter at the carrier in Evie's hands. "A feline, you say?"

"That's what Mom said," Evie said.

Belladonna stared at the carrier, studying it from all angles with contortionist twists of her head. Her tail twitched once, twice, and her wary eyes blinked. After a long, scrutinizing sniff, the cat uttered a cautious "Fine."

I raised an eyebrow. "Fine?"

"Yes. Fine. A cat is different. That I might be able to work with. Bring the creature forth so I may see if it's worthy of conversing with someone like me."

I resisted the urge to roll my eyes in exasperation, not wishing to provoke Belladonna's wrath further by appearing insolent. Her irritable temper seemed poised to erupt at the slightest provocation, and an ill-timed eye roll or look of impatience would likely stir her simmering pot of anger once more.

Another outburst of indignant rage was the last thing we needed.

Evie set the carrier on the floor and unlatched the door.

Nugget poked her head out cautiously, calico fur a mix of ginger, black and white. She meowed warily at the sight of Belladonna peering down at her from the platter like a wrathful pagan goddess atop a mountain.

"A calico." Belladonna sniffed. "How pedestrian. Very well, let us see if this simple little triple-colored tart has anything useful to share. You may proceed with your inquiries. I shall go over there and watch the dimwitted furball lower my platter's IQ."

"Wow, she's really in a mood," Evie whispered.

Belladonna froze, her face caught in an exaggerated look of offense, black paw poised theatrically mid-step down from the cubby. She whipped her head around to pierce Evie with an indignant stare, tufted ears shoved forward like blades seeking a new quarrel. "What did you say?" she hissed, rasping as sharply as a claw on a chalkboard.

Evie offered Belladonna a friendly smile, even in the face of her obvious agitation. "Nothing," she replied innocently.

Belladonna's bushy tail twitched once in warning, as if hoping for an excuse to continue her tantrum. I could see that the slightest sound from Evie might set her off again—her claws flexing in and out as if preparing to dig in for another dramatic tirade. "Are you sure you said nothing? I thought I heard something."

"Nope. Nothing." Evie smiled. "Not a thing."

Belladonna narrowed her eyes.

Evie smiled wider.

Landon quickly raised a hand to cover the grin breaking out on his face, unable to contain his amusement at Belladonna's obvious annoyance over being outmaneuvered.

Belladonna's claws slid back into their sheaths as Evie's polite reassurances deprived her of an excuse to continue her tirade. With a hiss of displeasure at being thwarted, the cat lowered her puffed up sleek fur, glare sliding from Evie to me and back again.

"Love you, Bella," Evie told her.

Her tail lashed once in resentment, outraged by Evie's diplomacy outmaneuvering her tantrum. Defeated, Belladonna dropped onto her haunches, eyeing us with malevolence one last time. Finally, she grudgingly descended to the floor.

Evie placed Nugget on the platter in the cubbyhole.

The calico sniffed the glowing plate suspiciously, eyes round.

Evie smiled, speaking in a gentle, reassuring tone. "Once this platter starts glowing, you can speak with us through your thoughts. We'll hear everything you think, and you can talk to us. Go ahead. Try it."

A few heartbeats later, the platter began emitting its

familiar glow. Nugget was startled at first, then seemed to relax into it. Her eyes drifted half-closed in feline contentment. The cat meowed tentatively. "What... what happened to Harold?"

Evie's smile faded. "I'm afraid Harold had an accident. He's no longer with us."

Nugget's ears drooped. "He's gone?"

"He is. I'm sorry."

The cat closed her eyes but accepted the news with quiet dignity, as cats often do in the face of sorrow or loss. After a moment, Nugget opened them again, gazing at each of us in turn. "Who are all of you? Where am I?"

I offered the cat a reassuring smile. "This is a cat rescue."

"Am I in need of that?"

"Everyone needs that sometimes. I'm Ellie, and this is my daughter Evie, her boyfriend Matt, and my...friend, Landon. We had some questions for you about Harold, but..." I hesitated. "Since you didn't know he was hurt, does this mean you weren't at the store when Harold fell off the ladder?"

"Master Harold isn't the sort to fall from such a contraption," Nugget replied with certainty. "We played on it all the time."

I blinked.

Master Harold?

I may have blinked, but Belladonna's ears twitched, attuned to any hint of fresh intrigue that might demand her attention with a piercing stare or haughty interrogation.

She leaped onto the platter beside the other cat, her temper unexpectedly cooled. "Well, it's obvious this creature comes from good breeding and has been well-educated. Considering the circumstances, solitude is what she requires to properly grieve. Leave us." Without waiting for an argument, she shooed us off with an impatient paw flick. "Go on, off with you!"

We knew better than to argue with Belladonna's imperious commands. Confronting her would only lead to undignified retaliation and wounded pride we had no desire to provoke.

Landon, Matt, and I exchanged rueful glances and shuffled out in a disorganized line under the smug scrutiny of her watchful stare.

Evie started to follow, her step hesitating. She glanced back at Nugget on the glowing platter, worry etched into her young face, instinct urging her to remain. But Belladonna shot her a scathing look of warning to remind my daughter that sentiment had no place in the isolation room at present.

Reluctantly, Evie exited the room, pulling the door shut behind her as Belladonna looked after her with a gaze of pompous entitlement at this further evidence of her undisputed reign.

Chapter Three

BELLADONNA'S CRYPTIC COMMENTS AND SLY mannerisms were an enigma wrapped in a fur coat. Distracted, trying to decipher her behavior like some diabolical ancient code, we descended to the first floor only to find Deputy Markham and Officer Mario Lopez waiting for us in the shelter's foyer.

Markham's gaze swept over our group with sharp eyes that cataloged details and clues the way a magpie collects shiny trinkets. "Mrs. Rockwell, Mr. Rogers. Kids. We have some questions about Harold Goldfinch's cat and were hoping you folks might be able to provide a few answers. Lopez mentioned you have it?"

My mood took another nosedive at his formal tone—not to mention the grim lines etched into his weathered face. I glanced at Mario, who offered an apologetic shrug and half-smile as if to say Markham was in one of his intense, inquisitive moods, and there was no steering him from it.

"Of course, Deputy," I said, following his lead to keep it formal and respectful. "Please, come in. Can I offer you gentlemen some coffee or tea?"

Don Markham shook his head, glancing around the foyer with sharp eyes. "No need. This shouldn't take long. The calico. Did Mr. Goldfinch drop that off?"

I shook my head. "No, someone else brought the cat here. Evie saw the woman but didn't recognize who it was."

"The car was silver, though," Evie said.

"Was the cat hurt or acting strange when it came in?" Markham asked.

"Not that we could tell," Evie said. "Just seemed like a normal, healthy cat."

Markham's gaze swung to Evie. "You were the one who spoke with this person, correct? Can you describe them for me? Or tell me anything that stood out as strange about the interaction?"

Evie shook her head. "I'm afraid not, Deputy. There was no interaction. I didn't speak to the woman. She parked her car, ran up the walkway, dropped Nugget on the porch, and ran off before anyone could speak to her. I only saw her from the window. I never got a good look. I'm sorry I can't be of more help."

Markham sighed, scribbling notes onto a small pad he'd retrieved from his pocket. "No, I understand. Thank you." He slipped the pad back into his pocket and turned to Lopez. "Guess that's another dead end. Get any security footage they have. I'm going to look around the parking lot, and then we'll head back to the station. I want to go over the coroner's preliminary report again."

Lopez nodded. As Don Markham turned to leave, he glanced over his shoulder and offered me an apologetic look. "Sorry for the inconvenience. If you could, I'd like you to keep Nugget for the county until I say otherwise. I'll have Mario bring the paperwork over later this afternoon."

I smiled at him, clocking that he'd switched from formalities and the interrogator tone to friendly first names. "Of course, Don. We'll take care of her."

"I know you will." Deputy Markham glanced at Landon, tipped his hat, and walked toward the front door. Over his shoulder, he said, "You've got ten minutes, Lopez."

Well, mostly friendly.

Mario waved us over as soon as Markham had left, ushering us into the small office behind the reception desk. Once the door clicked shut, he leaned against the desk and sighed. "Sorry about Don. He's like a dog with a bone once he gets an idea in his head."

"It's fine, Mario," Landon said.

Mario scrubbed a hand over his face, glancing at each of us in turn. "The thing is, even Don admits everything points to this being a tragic accident. But he also says his gut's telling him something's hinky about it all the same."

I blinked. "Hinky?"

Mario shrugged. "Suspicious or off in some way."

"Can you really rely on a feeling that something's 'hinky'?" Landon asked.

"With Don Markham, sometimes. He's got good instincts. Not always the most tactful in following them, but his hunches usually pan out." Mario frowned. "I don't know. The wall ladder, no sign of a struggle, the cat disappearing… Don's right that we don't have any solid evidence proving this wasn't an accident, but there's a lot of weird going on." He looked at me. "Did Nugget say anything?"

"Not a thing," I told him. "All we know is she wasn't there when he fell."

Mario nodded slowly. "Without more concrete evidence, the county's calling this an accidental death for now." His gaze traveled over each of us, expression grim. "Which means this stays between us, got it? As you can imagine, I'm not really supposed to be telling you any of this."

We all nodded in agreement.

"So what now?" Evie asked.

Mario sighed again, dropping into the desk chair. "Now we keep looking for anything that proves Don's hunch right—starting with the security footage showing what happened when Nugget got dropped off here."

A fresh wave of sorrow and disbelief washed over me.

Harold Goldfinch dead.

My gaze drifted out the window to where his familiar blue sedan was usually parked during the morning coffee rush, the engine idling while Harold ran into the cat café to grab his daily coffee and paper.

The parking space stood empty now, and the grim notion that Harold Goldfinch's light may have been snuffed out ahead of schedule stuck in my head.

We gathered around the desk, jostling for position to peer at the small monitor displaying security footage from cameras positioned around the property. On screen, the feed from the front entrance showed a familiar view of the cat rescue's walkway and porch, capturing anyone coming or going through the main doors as well as a narrow glimpse of the adjacent parking lot.

There—a flash of silver caught the light as a nondescript sedan pulled into one of the parking spaces flanking the long drive leading out to the main road. The car was unremarkable, a generic four-door model that might blend into traffic anywhere. My breath caught as the driver's side door swung open, a figure stepping out into the camera's line of sight.

They were obscured from view by the hood of an

oversized jacket—in August in Texas—and a pair of sunglasses so large they seemed better suited for a movie star hiding from paparazzi than this unknown visitor.

Everything about their manner and appearance hinted at a desire to avoid detection. They seemed unconcerned with the security cameras—or perhaps unaware and overconfident in their attempts at anonymity.

The figure strode purposefully toward the front entrance, head on a swivel, ensuring they weren't followed or observed. They glanced once over one shoulder, peering down the drive leading back out with what seemed like calculating scrutiny, and then the porch obscured them from view.

"Can't make out any details with those glasses and that hood up," Landon muttered.

"Give it a minute," Mario said. "She's still far away."

We watched as the figure—a woman—strode purposefully up the walkway, a blue cat carrier clutched in one hand. She set it down upon reaching the porch, flipping open the latch to release the calico cat inside. The woman shook the carrier once impatiently, dislodging her reluctant passenger onto the welcome mat in a patch of orange, white, and black fur.

Her errand complete, the woman snatched up the now empty cat carrier and hurried off down the path as swiftly as she'd come. Not once did she glance back at the bewildered calico watching her retreat, climbing back into the silver sedan within seconds. The slam of her car door was followed shortly by the crunch of gravel under tires as she sped off down the drive without a backward glance.

"She didn't knock or ring the bell before leaving Nugget," Evie said with a frown. "And leaving her with no carrier? What a horrible person. Why not leave Nugget on the porch in a carrier?"

"Identification, maybe? Fingerprints?" Landon asked.

We watched the footage in silence as Nugget sat, confused, sniffing the air cautiously before looking around to survey her new surroundings. With a single meow, the cat stretched out in a patch of sunlight, tail flicking, now abandoned in a strange new place.

"No easy ID on that mystery woman. No license plate visible on the video, either," Mario said with a sigh. "Don's not gonna be happy about that." He looked up at me. "Did you all ask the cat about the woman yet?"

"No. Belladonna wanted some time with Nugget alone after we told her Harold had passed."

Mario looked at Evie. "Run it one more time?"

My frown deepened as we studied the footage again, searching for any small detail that might hint at the woman's identity or why she'd dropped Nugget off in such a hurried, impersonal fashion. "She seems nervous. In a rush to get out of here for some reason."

"Guilty conscience, maybe?" Landon suggested.

Mario scrubbed a hand over his face, expression troubled. "At this point, anything's possible. All we know right now is how strange this situation is—the accident that might not be an accident, Nugget showing up out of the blue, and now this mystery woman in a hurry to disappear again." When the video reached its end again, Mario pulled the flash drive disk from the computer and slipped it into his jacket pocket. "The county's on this, though, and they have a tech team. I'll see if they can pull any additional details or run facial recognition on the footage. Maybe we'll get lucky."

Matt asked, "Is there anything we can do to help?"

Mario sighed. "I'd like to talk to Nugget myself." He glanced at the closed door of the office. "I don't have a whole lot of time right now."

"That, and Belladonna tossed us all out for some reason," Landon told him.

A sly smile played at the corner of Mario's mouth as he eyed Landon. "You all take orders from a cat now?"

"No, we don't take orders from a cat," I said. "As eloquent as these furry primadonnas may be, we shouldn't forget they're animals, not humans. No matter how many snotty soliloquies Belladonna launches into, she's still just acting on instinct, agenda, and periodically, a burning desire for treats."

Mario snorted. "Right. My mistake."

"I'm not kidding, Mario."

His chuckle faded.

"Even before they could talk to us, cats didn't need us. They are creatures that require little care as pets. Unlike dogs, there's no training or grooming needed.

Cats are content to snooze the day away or prowl around without a second thought for us. They are secretive, aloof, vain, and thrive on their own terms even if they like you. They are enigmas, and you should never forget they have agendas. I don't know what Belladonna's is here, but you can rest assured she has one, and she won't tell us unless she's ready for us to know."

"Right." His amused expression sobered. "Okay, looks like I'm out of luck talking to Nugget for now. Guess that'll have to wait until Belladonna decides we're worthy to be in her presence again."

"She gets like this sometimes," Evie said. "She sulks. Or plots. Or whatever else she's doing."

Mario shook his head, chuckling quietly. "Never a dull moment around here, is there?" He straightened, expression turning serious once more. "I should head to the car before Don wonders what's taking so long. Let me know if you get anything more out of Nugget. And keep an eye out in case our mystery woman comes back."

"Will do," Landon said.

Landon and I stood side by side, watching the deputy's patrol car dwindle into the distance down the winding lane until it vanished from sight. An unwelcome sense of disquiet settled in my stomach as it disappeared around the bend, taking with it our chance at definitive answers—at least for now.

The mystery woman's dramatic entrance and swift ditching of Nugget like she was last season's handbag lingered at the forefront of my mind, her dubious motives and icy indifference lighting a fire of annoyance I couldn't extinguish with the entire contents of a Trenta Starbucks.

I glanced at Landon, whose expression resembled that of a philosopher trying to decipher the meaning of life, and figured similar thoughts must be doing jumping jacks on his brain as well.

Harold Goldfinch was dead.

Nugget had shown up with no explanation.

And now a suspicious woman on security footage, her identity and motives unknown.

Three pieces of a puzzle that didn't quite fit together. I sighed, gazing out at the cat rescue grounds where the usual midday activity seemed oddly subdued. It was like a feeling of unease had settled over the place like a pall.

"I don't like this," I murmured.

Landon's hand found mine, his fingers lacing tight through my own. "We'll figure it out." His eyes met mine, expression resolute. "Whatever's really going on here, we'll get to the bottom of it. We always do."

I could only hope he was right.

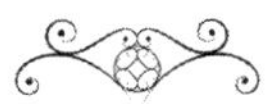

With Belladonna and Nugget safely contained in the isolation room for now, we did our best to carry on with the usual tasks at the cat rescue in spite of the strange events plaguing us. I threw myself into the familiar routine of chores and maintenance in an effort to keep my worries at bay, if only temporarily. Thoughts of Harold Goldfinch and Nugget receded to the back of my mind, as did speculation over the woman who had abandoned the cat so callously.

Landon glanced up from the calico cat snuggled content in his arms, Sundae's rumbling purrs of pleasure punctuating the relative silence. His hands worked in a steady, rhythmic motion down her back, earning an occasional meow of delight when scritching just the right spot.

"You're going to adopt that cat," I told him again.

Sundae stretched languidly under his gentle strokes, utterly relaxed and without a care as long as those hands kept lavishing her with affection. The calico's eyes had slid shut in feline bliss, her furry body limp with enjoyment of the attention.

"Naw, I'm over here too much, anyway. Speaking of which, I should get going soon," he said, tilting his head toward the front door leading to the parking lot. "That cabinet order's due by the end of next week, and I've barely started the sanding, much less the joinery."

It sounded like English.

I smiled, leaning over to scratch behind Sundae's ears. The cat purred loudly, leaning into my touch. "Sundae will definitely miss you."

"Just Sundae?" he asked.

Landon made no move to go just yet, though, continuing to lavish Sundae with attention until she decided she'd had her fill, leaping down from his lap with a trilling meow to pad off in search of her next amusement. He watched the calico go with a wistful half-smile, scrubbing a hand through his hair with a rueful chuckle. "Duty calls for us all, I suppose. These pieces won't build themselves, and clients wait for no man."

"Of course not. In fact, why don't you come over for dinner tonight? Evie saw an interesting recipe on VidVerse she thought she'd try and she'll have more than enough food. Whether it will be edible, I can't say. Some kind of exotic curry. Matt's staying for dinner, too."

He contemplated that, expression thoughtful. After a moment, Landon nodded. "Sure, I could do that. And, actually..." He hesitated, gaze searching my face. "There was something I wanted to talk to you about."

A flutter of nerves stirred in my stomach at his tone. "Everything okay?"

"Yes, everything's fine. It's just... earlier, when you called me your friend." He paused, brushing cat hair from his clothes, before looking up again. "Is that really all we are?"

Oh.

That.

Heat crept into my cheeks, and I suddenly busied myself straightening a stack of paperwork to avoid meeting his gaze. I was flustered by the question even though I knew my answer was totally reasonable.

"Ellie?"

"Of course, that's not all we are, Landon." I stopped

futzing. "But we're both in our fifties. 'Boyfriend' and 'girlfriend' sounds a bit juvenile at this point in our lives, don't you think?"

"You're sure that's all it was?" Landon pressed. "Just sounding ridiculous?"

I gazed up at Landon then, willing my expression into what I hoped passed for a reassuring smile. His searching look evidenced that my attempt had fallen short, doubts and worry still bleeding through the hastily erected facade.

"Of course," I reiterated, as much for myself as for his benefit. "What else could it be?"

His eyes remained on mine for a long, considering moment, thoughts obscured behind an unreadable mask. At last, Landon's attention shifted to the open doorway behind me, expression shuttering as he gave a short nod.

"Right. Okay, then." He scrubbed a hand through his hair, gaze darting back to me as if on impulse. "I should get going. See you tonight?"

"Absolutely. Around six work for you?"

"Six it is." Landon leaned in, brushing a soft kiss over my cheek that made my breath catch. "It's a date."

He turned and pushed through the front door to leave. I watched until the door closed and found myself alone in the shelter's foyer with only my troubled thoughts—and many cats—for company.

Chapter Four

The savory aroma of Evie's Chicken Tikka Masala wafted through the air as we sat around the dining table, mouths watering in anticipation of her latest culinary masterpiece. Steaming bowls of vibrant yellow rice and perfectly cooked vegetables accompanied the main dish, a blend of spices that filled the dining room with an exotic, enticing perfume.

"It looks fantastic, Evie," Matt told her affectionately.

Evie's face flushed with delight at the praise.

Landon lifted his wine glass. "To the chef. I'm sure it'll be amazing."

"To the chef!" Matt and I echoed, lifting our glasses.

Evie ducked her head, the pink glow flushing into a brighter red. "It's nothing too fancy. Just chicken, tomatoes, cream, and a few spices. The masala adds a nice savory kick, though."

"Smells fancy to me," Matt said, leaning over to brush a soft kiss against her cheek.

I lifted a bite of the saucy chicken dish to my lips, pleasantly surprised by the blend of flavors that blossomed on my tongue—savory yet mildly sweet, with a hint of heat from peppers and a robust warmth. "Delicious! The spices are perfect. You've outdone yourself, honey."

Landon eagerly spooned another bite of the fragrant Chicken Tikka Marsala into his mouth, savoring the blend of spices with a groan of pleasure. "There's a reason I never pass up an invite for dinner around here," he said, pausing just long enough to flash Evie an appreciative grin.

The heaps of well-deserved compliments left Evie radiating joy from ear to ear, her smile lighting up the room. She laughed, shaking her head. "Flatterer. You just like having a home-cooked meal, so you don't have to fend for yourself."

"Guilty as charged," Landon admitted without a shred of remorse.

"Did you manage to make any progress on those cabinets today?" I asked, taking advantage of a lull in enthusiastic bites. Landon's attention remained mostly focused on his plate, though he glanced up at the question.

"Not as much as I'd have liked. Got a late start." His tone was pleasant despite the mild complaint, as if he didn't truly mind. "I'll be putting in extra hours this week to make up the difference. My clients are usually pretty understanding, but I don't like falling behind."

"Matt could give you a hand this weekend if you need help catching up," Evie offered without bothering to check with her boyfriend. Landon's smile turned grateful, eyes softening at the thought.

"I might take you up on that. Many hands make light work, as the saying goes."

We slipped into an easy back and forth, lingering over the emptied plates and glasses as minutes stretched to hours while trading stories and jokes. My worries faded for a time as I watched Landon and the kids chat back and forth, and I felt buoyed by the warmth of good food, wine, and loving company.

Landon lounged back in his seat, arms folded contently over his stomach. I watched him and Evie debate the latest StreamFlix documentary they both watched, and the fondness rose up within me. His presence never seemed to fail to set the people around him at ease, and he so obviously delighted in life's simple moments.

Our lively dinner chatter and laughter abruptly stopped as the apartment wing's front door suddenly banged open. Veterinarian Laurie Gray came storming in, clutching one hand wrapped in a dish towel.

"Ellie, what did you do to provoke that little beast this time?!" Laurie shouted. She stomped over to the table, her eyes flaming in exasperation.

What do you mean, what did I do? I thought. I'm not the one bleeding here.

I cleared my throat, attempting to channel my inner Meryl Streep. "What furball? I haven't the faintest idea what you're referring to."

I knew very well what furball enigma she meant.

It was the same furball we were always discussing, the subject of many a lengthy meeting over margaritas and the cause of more than a few premature gray hairs. The tiny diva herself, her highness Belladonna—aspiring Bond villain extraordinaire and feline mistress of mystery.

Laurie waved her towel-wrapped hand under my nose as exhibit A, looking about as thrilled as someone who just found a cockroach in their oatmeal. "Belladonna! That furry little psychopath went full-on Hannibal Lecter on me when I checked on poor Nugget. Look what she did to my hand!"

We might need an exorcist at this rate to rein in her diabolical impulses.

Upon unwrapping the makeshift bandage, Laurie's hand resembled something straight out of a low-budget slasher film. The scratches weren't deep, but they were bloody and angry.

"Oh, no," I said, jumping up from my seat with an overly horrified expression. "I know now probably isn't the time to remind you that moving here was something you asked me for and not something I suggested. Using that plate in the isolation room on a near-daily basis? That genius idea was all you."

Laurie stared daggers at me, looking thoroughly unamused.

"Do those dramatic flesh wounds require stitches, or will a band-aid do the trick?" I asked. "Since you're an animal doctor, I imagine you know."

Her scowl deepened, annoyed, as Evie chuckled. "What?" Laurie asked her.

"You do have a tendency to storm in there like you're leading a SWAT team raid," Evie pointed out. "She doesn't like that. From her perspective, that room and that plate are her territory."

"Laugh all you want," Laurie scoffed. "But until you've come face to face with Hannibelladonna and her claws of death, you won't understand why stealth is not an option." She turned to me and thrust her arm out. "Honestly, Ellie, you need to do something about that cat. She's a menace."

"Hold still." Laurie winced as I examined the angry scratches. "You're fine. Just go wash your arm in the sink."

She did, calling through the doorway from the kitchen, "Ever since Fiona made her inheritance contingent on that cat's happiness, she's been nothing but trouble."

"I think she was probably trouble before that," Matt called back.

"Just not our trouble," Landon added.

Laurie was right that Belladonna had been difficult from the start—unpredictable and temperamental, hissing and scratching at anyone who crossed her for reasons known only to the cat.

Now, I would never toss out a difficult cat. But the fact that Fiona's inheritance and the rescue's non-profit operating budget were dependent on that animal's comfort and happiness (and decision to stay as opposed to run away) seemed to have amplified her less charming qualities, fueling a haughty belief in her own self-importance that led to frequent tantrums and outbursts.

Outbursts usually directed at Evie or me.

Well, and Laurie.

Laurie did insist on bringing dogs to the mansion, so I felt she incurred the wrath of Hannibelladonna with eyes wide open. Laurie knew the cat hated dogs, yet she played with fire anyway.

The woman had a death wish.

"Let me get the first aid kit and patch you up." I glanced at my daughter. "Evie, can you check on Nugget and Bella, please? Make sure they're okay."

Evie nodded and hurried off upstairs as I patched Laurie up. "You really need to find a way to make peace with you and Bella," I told her, opening the kit to gather bandages, antibiotic ointment, and gauze. "If you want to keep using the place, I think you need to keep that deal you made with her."

Laurie shook her head, biting her lower lip against the sting of ointment on her torn skin. "I have! I've given her the treats I promised her every time I brought the plate back from my office. I swear, I don't understand why she seems to hate me so much, Ellie—"

"You're a vet," Matt and Landon said simultaneously.

Laurie glared at the men.

"They're right. You're a vet, Laurie," I said, winding gauze around Laurie's hand to cover the worst of the scratches. "Most animals, in general, aren't very fond of their vet. However, there's no way to know with Belladonna unless she tells you. Her thoughts are her own, and you'll need to develop a rapport with her to find out what they are," I said as I grabbed the outer bandage. "Or you'll have to start wearing long sleeves with a tight weave."

"I can prescribe Xanax for her," Laurie said.

"Maybe you should prescribe that for you, and you can take it one hour before seeing her." I secured the end of the bandage, tying it off to hold the gauze in place. "There, that should do."

Laurie flexed her hand, wincing slightly at the pull against the bandage, then sighed in resignation. "These things happen. At least she didn't go deep enough I'd need stitches." She offered me a rueful smile. "You're right. I have no patience with her. I just barrel in and do what I need to do. I'll try to—"

"Mom!" The front door slammed again, and Evie rushed back into the room, eyes wide. "Mom, Nugget's gone!"

I blinked, certain I must have misheard. "What do you mean, gone?"

"Gone as in not there. There's no sign of Nugget anywhere!"

This couldn't be happening.

Not after the day we'd already had.

"Belladonna!" I shouted, pushing past Evie as I raced up the stairs. "Belladonna, where's Nugget? What did you do?!"

Silence greeted me as I burst into the room, confirming my worst fear.

The cat rescue's newest charge had vanished without a trace.

And Belladonna, it seemed, had gone with her.

Landon and I ran through the field behind the cat rescue calling Belladonna and Nugget's names. At least it was still daylight, allowing us to see what was happening, but as the sun dipped lower toward the horizon, our visibility window grew smaller.

"We have a court review next week, and if the judge can't confirm Belladonna's safety and care, we lose the rescue," I reminded Landon, panting slightly.

"I know, Ellie. We'll find them."

We'd been searching for nearly an hour, scouring every inch of the grounds to no avail. "If we don't, we lose the rescue." Swiping a hand across my forehead, I brushed away the beads of sweat that had formed. "I swear, Fiona must have known what a menace that cat could be to put a catch like that in her will. I will need therapy if this cat doesn't calm down."

Landon shook his head, chuckling despite the grim situation. "Fiona always did seem to find Belladonna's dramatics amusing, and that was before we all knew the cat could talk. Knowing that now, I have no doubt Belladonna had Fiona wrapped around her paw from day one. The two of them against the world."

A flash of movement caught my eye, and I gasped. "There!" I pointed toward the tree line, where two furry shapes were slinking through the underbrush. "Quick, before they disappear again!"

We took off running, but Belladonna heard our approach and hissed, nudging Nugget to scramble beneath a large log. The fallen cedars were like massive pickup sticks scattered behind the animal shelter, a perfect place for Bella and Nugget to hide.

"Bella, please stop!" I groaned in frustration, climbing over the moss-covered deadwood with Landon close behind, sweat beading on my brow from exertion and anxiety.

When we finally emerged on the other side of the log, Belladonna and Nugget sat primly in a small clearing as if waiting for us. But my attention was immediately drawn to the item on the ground between them—a canvas duffel bag emblazoned with the Goldfinch Coins logo.

Landon's eyes widened at the sight of it. "Is that—?"

I nodded. "It looks like it's from Harold's, yeah."

"Do we open it?"

I stared. "I don't think so. This is evidence in an ongoing police investigation. I mean, it is, right?" I frowned, mind racing.

Why had Belladonna led us here to find this? And how had she and Nugget known the bag from Goldfinch Coins was here? Did the lady that dropped her off this morning dump it here first? And why couldn't the darn cat just tell us instead of attacking Laurie and making a break for it?

As if in response to my unspoken questions, Belladonna meowed impatiently.

"Don't you sass me," I told her. "You may think I'm going to reward you for this, but not a chance. I don't know what game you're playing, but you better stop."

Belladonna hissed.

I turned to Landon. "What do you think?"

"Call Mario?" Landon asked. "I mean, we can't call Don. How would we explain to the deputy the cats lead us out here?"

"They got lost, we chased them?" Landon sighed, pinching the bridge of his nose. "Only in Tablerock," he muttered. His eyes met mine, resignation etched into his features. "Let's call Mario, let him know what happened. Let him decide what to do next."

I reached for my phone and dialed, bracing myself for questions from Mario that I couldn't answer.

The sound of tires on gravel alerted us to Mario's arrival. We turned to see his patrol car rolling to a stop near the clearing, the officer emerging with a frown, one hand resting instinctively on his hip near his weapon.

Though his expression was stony, I didn't miss the concern in his eyes as his gaze traveled over us, assessing for any sign of injury or distress.

"Where's the bag?" Mario asked without preamble.

I led him through the logs and into the clearing, pointing to the undisturbed duffel on the grass where we'd found it.

Mario's frown deepened as he took in the sight of it. Even from a distance, there was no mistaking the stenciled logo on its side.

Mario turned to us, eyes sharp, all business. "All right. Talk to me."

How did I even begin to explain this?

"We, uh, had an incident with Belladonna. She scratched Laurie and then ran off. I guess Nugget went with her, and we'd been searching for her and Nugget for a bit and spotted them running under that log. Then—"

"Slow down. Belladonna attacked Laurie?" Mario asked. "Is she okay?"

"Belladonna or Laurie?"

"Both, I suppose."

"Laurie will be fine. Just some cuts and bites,

nothing too deep. The cat is fine, too. But in the process of looking for the cats, we found that." I pointed. "We haven't touched it, and I think... well, I think they led us here on purpose."

"You do."

I nodded.

"Did the cats touch it?" Mario asked, suspicion creeping into his tone.

"I don't think so, but we can't be sure. They were in here for a while, and we couldn't see them." I took a deep breath, deciding blunt honesty was the only approach. "Look, it's a canvas duffel bag from Goldfinch Coins. Belladonna and Nugget led us right to it. If they were smart enough to do that, they were probably smart enough not to touch it."

"You think they wanted you to find it," Mario repeated quietly, swiping at a droplet of sweat rolling down his cheek. "Which means it's probably relevant to Harold's case in some way."

"Probably," Landon said.

"And so are they." Mario breathed in deeply and then breathed out. "Okay, let's back up. Explain in depth what led you here. Tell me everything."

Mario listened without interrupting, asking clarifying questions only occasionally with a curt nod or probing look at the felines that sat quietly at the edge of the clearing as if nothing in the world was going on.

By the time we finished relaying the events that had unfolded over this utterly surreal evening, full night had fallen, and the clearing was lit only by the beam of Mario's heavy-duty flashlight. "Right. So here we are."

"Here we are," Landon agreed.

Mario sighed again and approached the discarded duffel. "Only in Tablerock," he muttered, echoing Landon's earlier complaint. "Stand back. No telling what might be in here, but if Belladonna led you to find it, I somehow doubt it's anything good."

We did as asked, watching in tense silence as Mario knelt, snapped on a pair of latex gloves, and slowly unzipped the bag. His sharp intake of breath at what emerged from within made my heart clench in dread.

"What is it?" I asked.

"The Monterey Nugget," he replied (as if that clarified anything).

I blinked at him in confusion. "The who what now?"

"You're sure neither of you touched this bag?" Mario asked. When we shook our heads, he sighed. "Then it looks like our killer just made their first mistake. There may be prints or DNA on here we can use."

"Wait a minute. Now you think Harold was murdered?" Landon asked.

"I think stumbling upon a priceless artifact in the middle of a clearing we only found because of a cat that belonged to our dearly departed friend might indicate his untimely death was not quite the 'whoopsie daisy' it seemed. Call me skeptical."

"Well, when you put it that way," I muttered.

Belladonna raised her head at me, mouth curled in a

catty grin that looked suspiciously like a sneer of laughter. Nugget sat by her side, smug satisfaction rolling off both in waves.

"I don't even want to hear it," I told them.

Belladonna hissed again.

Mario set off through the brush toward his cruiser, already making calls to get forensics. Landon and I stood in troubled silence, gazes locked on the open duffel and its damning contents, a single thought echoing between us:

Why here?

What have we gotten ourselves into?

Chapter Five

THE HEAVY DOOR SWUNG OPEN AS LANDON AND I entered the isolation room, cats clutched in our arms meowing indignantly at their undignified treatment. We met each other's exasperated gazes over the furry forms of Bella and Nugget wriggling in our grips, and then deposited the two miscreants on the floor without ceremony.

Bella huffed, shooting me an irritated look as though I had inconvenienced her by interrupting her adventure. Nugget wasted no time scampering off to bat at the fringe of an ornate rug, her escape apparently already forgotten.

I crossed my arms, looming over the unrepentant tabby with a frown. "Would you care to explain how you got out of a locked isolation room and the building?"

Bella licked a paw nonchalantly, not deigning to justify her actions or appear even remotely apologetic.

Her calico counterpart paused in her play long enough to mewl cheerfully at Landon before pouncing on a stray feather fluttering by.

"Bella, I need to know how you escaped. This is serious."

Bella sauntered over to the talking plate cubby, exaggeratedly stepping on it. She held my gaze as the glow fired up, a challenge evident in her stubborn refusal to look away.

A firm answer rang out in the silence. "No."

"No?" I repeated, torn between laughter and exasperation.

Bella maintained eye contact for a second longer, as if to ensure her message had been received. Then she casually stepped off the plate, dropping to her haunches to groom her paw as though nothing important had occurred.

"Please tell me they're not all like that," Landon pleaded, glaring at the feline diva.

I shook my head, wanting to reassure him. "No, I'm certain Belladonna is one of a kind—she's in a class by herself."

"Advanced Theatrics and Manipulation 101?" he asked.

"Hey, Mom, you done?" Evie called up the stairs from reception office.

I poked my head out the door, spotting Evie. "We'll be right there!" I called down to her.

I turned back to Bella, catching her gaze with a stern

frown. "No more chaos or trouble from you tonight. No attacking anyone else. No leaving the mansion." Bella's ears flattened, whiskers twitching in irritation. I pressed on, refusing to be swayed by her show of defiance.

"No walks in the garden. No more manipulation or mischief." Bella hissed, displeased with this edict but I stood firm against her baleful glare, raising one finger in final warning. "We will discuss your behavior tomorrow. Am I understood?"

Bella sniffed, slinking off to curl up in a resentful ball of fur on her favorite window seat. I nodded, satisfied for now, and stepped out of the room after Landon. The lock clicked into place, sealing our mischievous charge in for the remainder of the evening under house arrest.

Hopefully.

Landon sighed, raking a hand through his hair. "Well, that was an adventure."

The aroma of freshly brewed coffee greeted us as we descended the stairs. Evie's face peeked out from the kitchen. "Everything all right now?" she asked, handing each of us a steaming mug. "It's decaf."

I took my first fortifying sip of coffee, feeling tension ease from my shoulders. "For the moment, it's fine."

"How did they get out?"

"I have no idea," I laughed shortly, the sound tinged with fatigue and grudging resentment of life with our challenging feline dictator. "And I doubt she'll ever bother to tell me, either. We need to do a sweep of the whole place. She couldn't have teleported through a wall."

"Tomorrow, then. I'll talk to Matt." Evie sipped her coffee. "You won't believe this, but Harold Goldfinch was a TubeTrekker. He had his own channel and everything. He just posted a video about the Monterey Nugget last week."

"What?" I blinked at my daughter in surprise.

Evie waved us over. "Come see for yourselves."

We hurried into the office where Matt sat at the computer. Evie, Landon and I crowded behind Matt's chair as he pulled up Harold's TubeTrek channel and clicked on the most recent video. It was dated the beginning of last week.

An image of Harold Goldfinch appeared on the screen, standing behind a display counter in his coin shop.

"Good afternoon, fellow numismatists and history buffs!" Harold greeted us with a broad smile. "Today I have a real treat to share with you. This"—he lifted a gold coin from the counter, holding it up to the camera with gloved hands—"is an extremely rare 1849 California gold rush era coin known as the 'Monterey Nugget.' It was one of the first coins ever minted in California to commemorate the discovery of gold at Sutter's Mill."

The coin featured a crude image of prospectors panning for gold in a river, with the words "Monterey Nugget—1849" etched around the edge.

"I recently acquired this coin from a widow's collection for a mere pittance. It is believed to be one of only three known surviving specimens. The coin is made of roughly 22-karat gold and about the size of a half dollar." Harold flipped the coin over, showing the back side. "As you can see, it has five small nuggets of native California gold stamped into the back, which is how it earned the name the 'Monterey Nugget.'"

"Who brags about screwing over a widow?" Landon asked.

"Harold Goldfinch, apparently," Matt said.

Harold went on to provide additional history about the coin, but I found it hard to focus on his words. My mind was reeling.

This couldn't be a coincidence.

The Monterey Nugget had been found dumped on our property, and now here Harold was presenting that same rare coin in a video posted just before his death.

I reached out and hit the space bar, pausing the video. "Harold must have been killed because of that coin. He broadcast that video advertising he had it, and less than one week later, he was dead. I mean, that can't be a coincidence."

Landon frowned. "But the coin was dumped. If someone killed him for it, why get rid of it?"

"Maybe the thief didn't intend to kill Harold," Matt suggested. "Maybe when Harold died, the thief freaked out and dumped the coin. They could have been intending to come back. Or maybe they changed their mind after the whole thing went south."

Evie shook her head, incredulous. "But the cat... Why would someone looking to steal a famous coin take the time to dump the cat at a shelter? That alone tells me it had to be someone who knew Harold—or Nugget—well. And who liked cats."

"Or we could have it backward," Landon pointed out. "Maybe they stole the Monterey Nugget after killing Harold to make it seem like a theft when it wasn't."

"You think Harold's death wasn't about the coin at all?" I asked.

Landon shrugged. "I don't know. But if he was murdered and the killer went to the trouble of staging Harold's death to appear accidental, dumping valuables tied to the crime points to a reason someone wanted him dead, and it wasn't money or a coin."

"That's a lot of ifs," I told Landon.

"I don't think the coin and cat were dumped as misdirection." Evie tilted her head, considering. "That pile of branches is way out on the corner of the Wardwell property. No one ever goes there. No one would have found that bag if it wasn't for Belladonna and Nugget."

"I mean, flip a coin here. Any of this is possible." Landon sighed, raking a hand through his hair. "There's only a few things we know. We know the coin and cat were dumped. We know Harold released a video to the world advertising he had the coin. Let's narrow it down. What doesn't fit? What's out of place?"

"The cat doesn't fit," Matt said decisively. "Why take Nugget at all? Dumping her here almost guarantee the police would have questions. It might even provoke a search of the shelter grounds. It doesn't make sense."

We sat in troubled silence for a long moment, possibilities churning in each of our minds. Finally, Landon cleared his throat.

"We need to tell Mario about this video. He should know Harold was advertising his possession of that coin right before he died."

"They probably know already, don't you think?" Evie asked.

Landon arched his eyebrow. "Better safe than sorry."

"Landon's right." I said. "This could be important evidence."

"I still can't believe Harold had a TubeTrek channel," Evie said, shaking her head. "He never seemed the social media type. I wonder why Mabel never mentioned it. I would see her over at the ice cream shop; she was always on her Pictogram. You'd think she'd link to a TubeTrek."

"Maybe he didn't feature her." Matt shrugged.

Landon's gaze sharpened. "Or maybe she wasn't as enthusiastic about working for him as she pretended to be in that parking lot."

"Dude, seriously?" Evie asked him.

"Are you suggesting Mabel could be involved?" I

asked. The idea seemed far-fetched, but we had so little to go on, any theory was worth considering. "Harold's loyal assistant of over twenty years?"

"I hope she's not," Evie said ominously.

"She's been by his side for decades, watching him get rich as a renowned coin dealer while she likely earned peanuts in comparison," Landon said, warming to the possibility. "Harold was set to retire soon. What if Mabel felt she deserved more for her years of service and made demands Harold refused? Opportunity, motive, means—she had all three. And she wouldn't want to see anything happen to the cat when the police arrived."

As I warmed up my before-bed tea, I had to admit Landon made a fair point.

Mabel was uniquely poised to catch Harold off guard and would potentially know how to make his death appear an accident. She also had an emotional attachment to Nugget.

And, I frowned, she seemed to know when she drove up something happened to Harold—even though the store was in a shopping center, and the paramedics and coroner could have been there for anyone.

I gestured to the tea cups lined up ready to be filled. "Evie, could you pass me that mug for Landon?"

Evie sniffed, eyeing the mugs with disdain. "Perhaps

a beer would be more to the liking of a knuckle-dragging Neanderthal."

"A knuckle... a what?" I froze, teapot in hand as I stared at her in shock. Where had that petty and uncharacteristic insult come from? "I...beg your pardon?"

"I feel like the local Tablerock water supply must be spiked with misogyny juice or something, considering how male minds work here." She glared at Landon as if he were solely responsible for global patriarchal oppression.

"Come again?" he sputtered.

My eyes narrowed, searching her face for clues to explain this sudden shift in her usually courteous demeanor. I handed Evie a mug of tea, wondering what she had worked herself into a feminist fury over now. "Here, and maybe take a sip. It'll calm you while you explain why you insulted Landon."

"Thank you," she said, and then turned toward Landon. "When Beau died, the cops hauled in Fiona faster than you can say 'witch hunt.' When Ben Tyson kicked the bucket, they immediately gave his girlfriend the stink-eye despite no evidence that she did anything. Everywhere else, the police seem to realize violent crimes are statistically more likely to have been committed by men—90 percent of the time, in fact. Except, I guess, in Tablerock, Texas, where the women are always under suspicion."

"Have you been getting into that new smokable hemp they're selling in Austin, or did we miss the announcement of 'Rally Against the Patriarchy' day?" I asked, hoping humor might defuse the situation.

"Evie, every living soul who's seen that rescue security footage agrees a woman was involved. That's the sole reason Mabel even came up in my mind," Landon explained. He spoke as if trying to reason with an unstable escapee from the feminism unit, afraid sudden movements might trigger a bra-burning protest.

It was like watching Steve Irwin calmly explain to a hissing cassowary why their territory was being invaded.

"Well, sure, there's that," she said slowly. "But you have no reason to think Mabel's loyalty to Harold is anything other than genuine. She lived and breathed to assist him. I don't like that you just jumped to these conclusions with no evidence—like that's what you think about women."

His eyes rose to meet mine at last. In their shadowed depths, I saw not anger at the slight to his pride or dignity, but anguish that he had somehow given my daughter cause to view him so.

At last he sighed, some of the tension leeching from his shoulders. "Evie, I apologize. I didn't mean to imply Mabel must be guilty just because she's a woman. I was spit-balling theories, and you're right that I should avoid acting on biases I may not even realize I have." He sighed, raking a hand through his hair. "My point was less about her gender and more that she's worked at that store for twenty years, yet she never seemed to share in its success financially. But you're right, that alone doesn't make her a killer."

Evie's glare eased, though she didn't seem fully mollified. "Well, as long as you understand why that assumption was problematic."

Landon nodded. "Duly noted. I'll do better at looking past stereotypes to consider all possibilities objectively." He offered her an apologetic smile. "Still friends?"

Evie sighed, then relented with a nod. "Friends. Just watch yourself, bub." She punctuated the warning with a pointed finger.

Landon held up his hands again and chuckled. "Yes, ma'am."

After everyone left for the evening, I settled into bed with Belladonna, Nugget, and my tablet. Landon's words about Mabel kept turning over in my mind, and before I could second-guess the impulse, I looked up her home address.

As the information populated, I blinked in surprise.

My search for traces of Mabel's life in Tablerock revealed a humble existence.

Mabel lived alone in a sparse rural apartment, barely able to make ends meet. I found a bankruptcy from several years ago. Though she had spent all her time helping Harold at his shop and that shop had done very well for him, financial security had eluded her. It appeared decades of tireless work had earned her cramped, isolated living quarters and long hours.

I found post after post from her stating she would be at the shop for a customer when it opened, and when it closed—but if she ever voiced a word of complaint, I couldn't find any posts detailing it.

She must have watched Harold gain fortune and status over the decades, building an empire and legacy she had played an integral role in creating—yet reaping few rewards or recognition for her efforts. Constantly on the sidelines, supporting the success of another from a distance.

Considering Harold had no qualms swindling helpless widows out of priceless heirlooms to expand his treasure trove, exploiting his fellow man for personal gain clearly kept him up at night as much as Belladonna pondering world peace kept her up.

Which is to say, not at all.

It painted a poignant picture I found hard to reconcile with my impressions of Mabel thus far. She'd always seemed so cheerful, helpful, and devoted to her work at the coin shop on the few occasions I'd had to talk to her.

But beneath the surface, I wondered now what private struggles or resentments she battled, and whether Landon's proposed theory held more merit than I wanted to consider. Had years of being taken for granted and under-appreciated finally taken their toll?

And considering all this, could any of us really blame her?

I glanced at Belladonna sitting primly at the foot of the bed and sighed. "You and I are having a talk tomorrow. I'm too tired to argue with you today, but running out of the house the way you did was dangerous. You can't do that."

Belladonna gazed back at me, utterly unrepentant.

I shook my head. "Aw, cat, there are coyotes out there, you know. You know what a coyote is? A wild canine with big teeth that would be more than happy to snatch you up for a snack. You nearly gave me a heart attack today with that little stunt."

Nugget's fur bristled at the mention of the coyote, her usually melodic meow strained with anxiety. She walked up the bed, paws kneading the blanket until she was nestled tightly into my side. She buried her face in my arm as if it were a hiding spot, a shelter from the coyote's potential jaws.

"See, Bella? This is a normal reaction."

If Belladonna was concerned, she didn't show it. She yawned, stretching out on the blanket across my feet as if my warnings were of no consequence.

I rolled my eyes at her nonchalance. "You may not care, but I do."

Nugget's rumbling purr oscillated between contentment and distress as I brushed my fingers through her downy fur.

"Don't you listen to her, and don't you worry," I told

Nugget, nodding toward the cat at the foot of the bed. "She may think she's invincible, but one of these days her recklessness will get her into real trouble. You stay in the shelter, and nothing can get you in here. I promise."

Nugget meowed again and butted her head against my hand, soliciting more petting and ear scratches. I obliged, shaking my head at Belladonna once more. She had lived up to her name today, causing chaos and distress, but I knew better than to expect an apology.

She did as she pleased and expected the world to fall in line.

At least Nugget seemed to understand, seeking me out for reassurance and protection from perceived dangers—real or imagined. I gave the anxious feline an extra cuddle, happy to provide comfort as I settled in for sleep.

Chapter Six

THE NEXT MORNING AFTER BREAKFAST, I MARCHED toward the isolation room with the grim determination of a prisoner facing the firing squad, bracing myself for the upcoming inquisition. The cat would be ready, claws sharpened and a Cheshire grin upon her furry face, I knew—prepared, no doubt, to bat around my psyche like a cat toy.

"Good morning again," I said, pushing the door open.

Belladonna sat prim and proper on her enchanted cat dish like a haughty queen holding court, piercing me with a gaze that would make the Sphinx seem an open book. The furry fiend was poised and ready, tail flicking as she watched me, eager to begin today's round of mental gymnastics.

"How was breakfast?" I asked.

She sat motionless, tail curled around her feet,

regarding me silently. The plate glowed and pulsed around her, indicating the refusal to answer was a choice.

I pulled out a chair with a scrape and sat, bracing myself. "Okay, Belladonna, look. This hostility has got to stop. We can't go on like this."

As Belladonna watched in stone-faced silence, Nugget wove between my feet, purring encouragement.

"This resentment seems to have escalated lately, and I can't believe this is any more fun for you to live with than it is for me. What's going on? What really happened last night?"

Belladonna remained motionless, giant eyes unblinking. Her tail twitched once where it lay curled around her, the only outward sign she heard my appeal.

Nugget meowed softly at Belladonna and planted herself at my side, a calico sentry standing guard against the black cat's icy indifference.

Belladonna hissed at the floofy cat.

But then she spoke.

"I wished to venture outside for fresh air and take a turn about the gardens. It appeared an entertaining prospect. One does grow dreadfully bored being cooped up inside all day with nary an amusement in sight, you know."

"*Nary an amusement* in sight? We're a shelter, Belladonna," I pointed out. "We have more cat toys than the Creature Comforts pet store, and Landon built three catios right off the café. You can go outside any time you want."

She continued as if I hadn't spoken. "My delicate constitution requires stimulation from time to time, and a spot of outdoor revelry and gaiety, weather permitting, of course, is just the ticket to lift one's spirits after being trapped indoors with the same dreary company day after day. That dreary company, by the way, is you." Belladonna yawned, unconcerned by my concern and perfectly comfortable prioritizing her ennui and selfish whims. "In short, it's how I chose to entertain myself yesterday."

I leaned forward, hands open in entreaty, hoping my sincerity might thaw her suspicious facade even for a moment. I hoped the olive branch could penetrate where words had failed before—but my mouth ran away with me. "Entertaining? You call attacking Laurie and worrying us half to death entertaining?" I shook my head. "Your antics are going to be the death of me. And running off like that—there are coyotes around here. What if one of them got you?"

"Assaulting the vet was merely an unexpected perk," Belladonna scoffed with a yawn. "That woman is a menace to feline society."

"Belladonna!" I sputtered, her blasé reply adding fuel to my temper.

"What?" She gazed at me, the picture of innocence. "She is well aware this cat still has claws and chooses to provoke regardless. Barging in here without care, disrupting my peace—"

"You're utterly impossible, you know that?" I threw my hands up, outmaneuvered once more. There was no reasoning with her selfish whims and haughty airs. I turned to Nugget, so far the lone voice of reason in this leonine bedlam. "And you! Why didn't you speak up about that coin?"

Nugget jumped onto the platter beside Belladonna, her ears drooping in distress. "I'm sorry. I didn't want to get in trouble, and I didn't think anyone would get hurt. I should have told you about that right away."

She then jumped down and padded over to me, bumping her head against my hand and meowing anxiously, soliciting forgiveness.

Well, isn't she sweet, poor thing.

I sighed, scratching her behind the ears. At least someone around here grasped the gravity of the situation. "Just don't let it happen again, okay?"

Harmony restored, she butted her head into my waiting hand with a trill of contentment and then meowed again while nudging my hand for more petting and reassurance.

Belladonna, on the other hand, remained utterly unrepentant, gazing back at me with bored indifference.

"Nugget," I said with a scritch, "do you have any idea who brought you here to the shelter?"

Nugget's ears drooped again, and she jumped back to the cubby hole. "No, I don't. I was taking a little nap in the little room at the store where all the stuff is kept when somebody came in. They threw a soft blanket over me and put me in a small, closed-up place. At first, I didn't worry because it felt like a little box. Boxes are the best places to be, so warm and snuggly. But then the box moved, and I didn't like it anymore."

"Could you see out?"

"Not really."

"Don't worry," I told her gently. "You're safe here now. I promise that no one will put a blanket over you or shove you into boxes against your will again." I scratched her head. "How did you know where the coin was, though? If you couldn't see out of the carrier you were in?"

"I peeked out from under the blanket," the little calico cat said, puffing out her chest proudly. "I saw where we stopped through the little crack in the blanket, and I told Bella. She said she knew where the big tree place was and could take me there, so we went."

The two cats chirped at each other, obviously pleased with their joint success.

"How did you get out of the shelter?" I asked.

Belladonna hissed, ears flattening against her skull, as Nugget cowered under the black cat's warning.

"Belladonna!"

Fur on end, the black cat swatted out a paw, and it snapped back just short of Nugget's nose. The poor calico shrank back as though struck (even though she wasn't) and scurried off the talking plate to hide behind the refuge of my chair legs.

I closed the door on the chaos within, pulse still rattling from the turmoil that cat seems to stir up in seconds. Belladonna's mood whiplash left me dazed as ever, and I was furious that she wouldn't tell me how she got out of the manor. That cat needed a therapist and possibly a padded cell.

Were there cat psychologists? Feline mental institutions equipped with scratching posts and mood stabilizers to wrangle hysterical black cats?

I snorted, shutting the fantasies away with the closed door.

Cat therapy and medications were the stuff of imagination—I was on my own (well, sort of) wrangling Belladonna and her outsized, unpredictable emotions, and I knew it. While other cat shelter founders enjoyed civilized lap cats, leisurely bonding, and the gratitude of a life saved, I would play cat and mouse with a tiny tyrant more suited to scheming world domination than napping the day away without a care.

Mario approached in a cloud of frustration, his habitual cheer erased by a fierce scowl. He shook his head as if to rid himself of excess anger before speaking.

"I just came from breakfast with Landon. He'll stop by later, but I wanted you to hear it from me first," he said, tension ringing through each syllable. He kept his volume low, but the words snapped like a whip, anger barely restrained behind the even, forceful cadence. "The Sheriff isn't buying it. According to Markham, our esteemed elected law enforcement boss is convinced Harold's death was just a tragic accident, and he thinks we're all wasting our time."

Evie, who'd followed Mario up the stairs, snorted at this proclamation, never one to mince words. "The Sheriff is a buffoon. That bumbling excuse for a cop couldn't solve a crime if the perpetrator confessed and provided video footage." Each word cast ripples of outrage.

"I didn't make the call, Evie. Don't unload on me like you did on Landon. I'm not in the mood for it." Mario was obviously hoping to avoid a possible rant over the patriarchal justice system and its many flaws. "We know Dixon struggles with connecting the dots, but until someone provides evidence to the contrary, that's where we're at."

I shook my head. "Even with that coin being dumped on our property?"

"Yep. Even so." Mario sighed at my expression. "Look, I know. I get it. Markham's not happy, either. But without concrete evidence of foul play, his hands are tied. Markham's a bit more open to foul play—he thinks maybe someone witnessed the accident or found the body after the accident, knew about the coin, and stole it to make it look like Harold was killed for it."

"That man can make mountains out of molehills. That's ridiculously complicated." I shook my head adamantly. "It makes no sense unless the person that found the body killed Harold. I mean, right? Come on, Mario, even you have to admit that sounds insane."

"I don't—"

"Exactly," Evie said, cutting him off. "Did you even check for security footage at the store? I find it hard to believe a coin shop wouldn't have cameras."

Mario nodded. "There were cameras. But the footage for the day of Harold's death is gone. The system was wiped clean."

I stared at him, a deluge of frustration uncorked by that one small, ominous question. "Are you kidding me?"

His pause belied the full force of invective clenched behind his teeth. "I know," he said. "Blame the voters. The sheriff makes the call, and he isn't interested in looking into it any further."

Law enforcement in our county followed an odd patchwork of jurisdiction. The Tablerock police represented the long arm of local law, hired or appointed by the city council and manager to keep just our streets in line.

But the county sheriff's department roamed wider, able to stick their noses wherever they fancied within the county limits, even right into our little municipality.

And their leader, Sheriff Bob Dixon, answered only

to the voters who elected him every few years—no city council oversight, approval, or experience needed.

And Sheriff Bob Dixon was… well, misguided would be a kind way to say it.

Power-hungry and lazy would be an unkind way.

"Someone deleted the footage, and the sheriff still thinks this was an accident?" I asked, not really expecting an answer. "Come on—that alone indicates this was no accident."

"I hear you. I do. But without that evidence, we have nothing solid to go on," Mario said. "The sheriff wants concrete proof of wrongdoing before devoting more resources to the case, especially with upcoming elections. I'm local, so I can keep digging, but it won't be long before Chief Yarbin will tell us to stick a fork in it, especially since the death will be ruled an accident and the county doesn't much care." He grimaced. "Politics."

"Has anyone checked if Sheriff Bob Dixon can tie his own shoes or just keeps Velcro straps around for convenience? Good grief, no wonder they need volunteers doing their jobs!" Evie huffed.

"I know." Mario shook his head. "My hands are tied unless we find something more substantial. I'm sorry."

We stood in troubled silence, the revelation settling heavily over us. The case seemed destined for the cold files before it had truly begun, and justice for Harold was no closer within our grasp.

The bell above the downstairs office door tinkled cheerfully as Darla escorted the visitor inside. I glanced up from the paperwork I was half-heartedly sorting through, startled to see Blanche Goldfinch, Harold's wealthy widow, walking toward me in her embroidered ivory dress and ropes of pearls. Her heels clicked decisively on the wooden floors as she approached the desk where I sat.

Blanche's eyes were puffy and rimmed with pink, evidence of the tears she had shed. But her stride was steady, hands clasped before her in a white-knuckled grip. She held herself with a forced composure that spoke volumes about her internal anguish.

Darla met my questioning gaze, murmuring under her breath as they approached. "Mrs. Goldfinch is here to pick up Nugget. I thought... under the circumstances, it would be better if you handle talking to her about what's going on with the cat." She offered an apologetic shrug before returning to the reception area.

Blanche and I moved in the same social circles, familiar faces at community events and fundraisers. We would exchange pleasantries over the fruit punch, commenting on the weather or the newest items on display at the silent auction. Sometimes, we would venture deeper than those cordial superficialities if we had enough time and privacy. Our distant friendship lingered just below the surface, though, never really risking a deep plunge into more personal waters.

There was nothing like death, though, to churn a storm.

"Blanche, I am so sorry about Harold." I reached for her hands, oddly frail in my gentle grasp, and led her to the armchair tucked in the corner. "Please, have a seat. Is there anything I can do?"

"No. No." Blanche sat, dabbing at her eyes with a tissue. "I'm sorry for the state I'm in. I just..." She sighed. "I'm not surprised Harold died in that store, you know? He was always there. I couldn't get him to leave if I tried."

"I understand." I nodded.

"Too much dedication, if you ask me." Blanche shook her head. "And now look where it's gotten him." She frowned, composing herself again. "Forgive me. I don't mean to burden you with all this. I'm having trouble keeping myself together today. It's all just so sudden. And now, with that coin found on your property —I just don't understand what's happening. Not at all."

"This must be so confusing for you. I'm always here to listen if you need it," I said, and then I hesitated—torn between my desire to comfort her as a friend would and my curiosity to probe for details on the investigation.

But why choose when I could have my cake and eat it, too?

"I hope the police haven't caused you too much distress with their questioning." I kept my tone light, hoping my concern seemed sincere and not a thinly veiled attempt to pry into the state of their inquiries. "I spoke to Mario earlier, and there seems to be so much confusion."

Blanche waved a hand. "The sheriff seems more interested in closing the case than solving it, if I'm honest. As for Mabel and her theatrics..." She rolled her eyes. "Always the drama queen, that one. She acted as if she were the grieving widow, not me. And that coin —Mabel claims it belongs to her, but Ross Massey, Harold's lawyer? He claims Harold promised it to him before he died. Harold's brother just came into town and is muscling in everywhere. I can barely find privacy in my own home."

"Harold's brother?"

"His younger brother. Anton Goldfinch," Blanche said. The name must have been sour as a lemon on her tongue because she grimaced as if tasting something bitter. "He's a professional poker player. Flew in from Vegas on the red eye."

I cleared my throat delicately. "By the way, about Nugget—the shelter was asked to hold onto her for the time being while the police conduct their investigation. I hope that won't be an issue? If it is, though, I can call Deputy Markham and see if that hold has expired." She just stared at me. "She's doing all right. Nugget is."

Blanche sighed again but nodded. "As long as she's well cared for, Nugget can stay as long as needed. It might be a good idea since the cat lived at the shop and has never been at the house before. With everyone traipsing in and out, Nugget could get spooked." She managed a wan smile. "At least I know she'll be looked after properly here. You've always done right by cats."

The cat had never been in Harold's house before? "We do our best."

"Besides, as I said, we've never gotten along, Anton and I." Her voice was flat, clipped. She glanced away, jaw tight, and I could glimpse years of tangled history and hurt swirling in her eyes before she blinked it quickly away. "The energy at the house just isn't good right now," she said. Gazing down at her hands, she rubbed her thumb over her knuckles. "Cats are so sensitive to that kind of thing."

I waited for her to ask to see Nugget.

She didn't.

She stood up. "I guess I should get back."

At the door, I placed my hand on Blanche's shoulder. "If there's anything else we can do for you or Nugget while you're going through this, don't hesitate to call. Even if you just need someone to talk to."

Giving her shoulder a reassuring squeeze, I offered a small smile.

Though her eyes were still clouded with worry, she managed a small nod in return. "You're too kind." Blanche patted my arm. "Give Nugget some extra love from me, won't you?"

"Of course. You have my word."

As Blanche departed, I slowly closed the door behind her and stared at it for a moment, my hand still on the knob. Somewhere in this town, the person who took Harold's life was walking free. I was sure of it, even if the police officially weren't sure of anything of the sort.

With a deep breath, I turned and went back to my desk.

The hunt was on.

Chapter Seven

THE SCENT OF ROASTED CHICKEN AND SIMMERING soups enveloped us as Landon, and I pushed through the door into Garcia's Corner Market the next morning. Grabbing a small handbasket, I made a beeline for the deli case, its glass fogged with the warmth of that day's freshly made meals.

"Blanche loves their meatloaf," I said, catching Landon's eye as he snagged two cold bottles of peach tea from a nearby cooler.

After grabbing a meatloaf and paying, we headed out the door. While nothing could completely lift Blanche's spirits, a home-cooked meal from her favorite market might warm her up, at least for an afternoon.

As we drove out to the sprawling Goldfinch estate, I sighed, the heavy events of the past few days weighing on my mind.

"I just don't understand how Sheriff Dixon can be so

dismissive about Harold's death," I said, frustration spilling into my tone. "That man wouldn't know a clue if it smacked him upside the head."

Landon nodded, his jaw tight. "I don't like to speak ill of people, but you're right. I've never seen a lawman more allergic to actual police work. I don't know how that man keeps getting re-elected."

"It's like he actively avoids solving anything substantial. Simple stuff? Sure, fine. Big, complicated stuff? That can't happen here," I huffed. "The security footage being deleted alone should raise all kinds of red flags."

"And you'd think a rare gold coin mysteriously appearing on the property of the cat shelter the deceased's cat was dumped at would pique his interest, but nope," Landon said.

"Ugh, I know." I thumped my palm against the steering wheel. "That buffoon couldn't find his way out of a paper bag with a map and a flashlight."

Landon chuckled. "Well, we'll serve the town as a map and flashlight then."

I smiled over at him. No matter how infuriating the situation, Landon always managed to buoy my spirits.

I eyed the road once more as I drove, the hum of the tires on the pavement the only sound between us. "Hey," he began, his voice soft. He turned in his seat to face me. "Everything okay with us?"

I darted a look at him, eyebrows raised. "Of course. Why do you ask?"

Landon lifted one shoulder in a slight shrug. "Just

checking in. I know you've seemed a little distant lately." He rubbed the back of his neck, gaze falling to his lap. "I wanted to be sure you're doing all right with this new step in our relationship."

When he looked back up, his brows were drawn together, forehead creased with concern. I reached over and gave his hand a reassuring squeeze.

"I'm good, really," I said. "It's just...an adjustment, going from being single for so long to being part of a couple. Don't get me wrong, I'm thrilled about us. But learning to lean on someone else more after handling things solo for years takes some time."

Landon nodded, threading his fingers through mine. "I get that. And I'm here for you whenever and however you need me. We'll figure out this relationship stuff together."

I took my eyes off the road momentarily to look at him. His shoulders were angled toward me, his body open and attentive. The morning sun lit up his face in a soft glow. "Thank you. Just knowing you have my back means the world," I said. "Now, let's meet Harold's poker-playing brother, shall we?"

As we neared the outskirts of town, I caught my first glimpse of the Goldfinch estate. My eyes widened at the sprawling mansion amid ten acres of meticulously manicured grounds. Perfectly pruned rose bushes and towering oak trees lined the half-mile-long driveway, not a leaf out of place.

"Fancy digs," Landon murmured.

"That's one way to put it." I craned my neck, taking in the imposing three-story manor. White pillars stood like sentries along the front porch, and elaborate flowerbeds overflowing with roses and hydrangeas surrounded a marble fountain.

We parked behind a shiny black BMW already in the driveway. As we got out, raised voices drew our attention to the manicured front lawn—I spotted a tall, broad-shouldered man in an open Hawaiian shirt and cargo shorts pacing as he shouted into his phone. "I need the lawyers here now! Before that gold-digging shrew my brother married destroys everything!"

"I hope that's not the brother," Landon murmured.

"I'm almost positive it is," I whispered back.

"Well, that's a shame," Landon whispered back.

Hawaiian shirt was gesticulating so wildly he looked like he was swatting flies, his face reddening like a tomato left too long in the sun. "I don't care what it takes. Just get them on the first flight out!" he bellowed into the phone.

I almost felt bad for the phone person on the other end, who was clearly getting an earful from an angry human tornado.

The grand front door opened, and Blanche hurried out, her face pinched with distress. "Anton, please!" she implored, wringing her hands. "The whole town can hear you." She quickened her pace across the manicured lawn, hair wisping in the morning breeze.

The whole town couldn't hear him, despite his impressive lung capacity. We were near the edge of town, and the property was large enough to swallow even his booming shouts (which were reminiscent of a deafening air horn).

Maybe he could be heard by the cows grazing in the next field over.

Maybe.

So this was Anton Goldfinch.

By the sound of things, Harold's estranged younger brother had arrived from Vegas quicker than a tumbleweed in a windstorm. And just as quickly, I understood the expression on Blanche's face the day before when she told me he'd arrived.

Speaking of Blanche, she spotted us walking across the driveway, meatloaf in hand, and hurried over like she was racing for the last lifeboat on the Titanic. Dark circles shadowed her eyes, making her look like a panda who'd forgotten to remove its makeup.

"I'm so sorry you had to see that little scene," she said, voice barely above a whisper. She shook her head, lips pressed in a thin line. "Ever since Anton arrived from Las Vegas, it's been nothing but drama around here."

I glanced over to where Anton was still shouting and pacing. "He seems pretty upset about whatever he thinks needs a ton of lawyers from Vegas to work out."

She leaned in, glancing back at her brother-in-law warily. "He says Harold promised he would inherit the coin shop and his entire collection of rare coins." Blanche sighed, a crease forming between her brows. "He also says Harold owed him a small fortune for some business they were planning to start together, or started together, or... I don't know. It's hard to follow it all."

"Well, I'm sure Harold had a will spelling out what he wanted, didn't he?"

"He didn't, actually. We had an appointment next week to start that process." Blanche looked embarrassed again. "I know, I know. We didn't have children, and we're married, so we just kept putting it off." She glanced at Anton. "I've told him repeatedly that Harold never mentioned what he's saying to me. But he insists Harold promised it all to him."

"Has he provided any proof of their agreement?" Landon asked.

"No, nothing concrete," Blanche said, glancing back at the house nervously. "Just a lot of shouting and accusations." She lowered her voice. "Between you and me, Anton has always had... money issues. Gambling debts, risky investments, you name it. Harold finally had to cut him off years ago, but I think Anton saw Harold's passing as a chance to try and get what he felt he was owed. He is his brother, and I don't want to ask him to leave, but..."

I worried if I poked Blanche, she might just tip right over. The poor thing seemed exhausted and stressed to the max, and I swallowed down a swell of anger on Blanche's behalf. To descend on her while she was still grieving, making demands, and causing scenes... it was unconscionable.

Anton ended his call at that moment and stormed toward the front door, face thunderous. Blanche paled, clasping her hands together tightly, nodding at the dish in my hands. "You're too kind to bring food, and I should invite you in, but I'm afraid now isn't the best time..."

"Of course, we understand completely," I said, handing the foil-wrapped meatloaf to her. "We just wanted to pay our respects and see if you needed anything." I darted a glance toward Anton's retreating figure, then leaned in close. Keeping my voice low, I searched her haggard face. "Blanche, I don't mean to pry, but are you safe here alone with him?"

"I think so. He wouldn't hurt me," Blanche said, though, from her tone, she might as well have said 'the Titanic will never sink.' "Well, physically, anyway," she added with a weak laugh. She straightened her shoulders, mustering a brave face like a soldier preparing to storm the beaches of Normandy. "I'll be fine. Harold's lawyer is coming by later to help me deal with all this."

I hoped Harold's lawyer was also adept at providing therapy and had plenty of wine on hand. Blanche was going to need all the help she could get.

"We can stay with you until the lawyer shows up," Landon offered.

"No, no. I'll be fine." Blanche managed a small,

grateful smile. "Thank you. Both of you. I appreciate your kindness more than you know."

"Please call us anytime if there's anything we can do to help," he added gently. "Day or night. We're here to help."

Blanche nodded, though it looked more like a bobblehead doll's head wobble. She then hurried back inside just as Anton burst out again, shouting anew into his phone with the ferocity of a wrestling announcer.

"Wow," Landon said as we walked.

"Yep. I agree."

As I slid behind the wheel of the car, we both turned to look back at the looming estate. Though muffled by distance, we could still make out the heated voices drifting from the front lawn. "It's mine! If you don't jump in here now and make sure I get my stuff, I will sue you! Do you hear me? I will sue you!"

Anton stomped like an angry toddler, huffing around the yard and waving his fists. If steam could actually billow out of ears like in cartoons, I had no doubt the poker player would be leaving mushroom clouds above his head right about now.

"Wow," Landon repeated again.

Anton's volatile presence cast an even darker cloud over the mystery surrounding Harold's death.

But it also gave us one more compelling suspect to consider.

Before we could put the car into gear to make our getaway, my hand froze on the gearshift as a police cruiser pulled up behind us, red and blue lights flashing. Out stepped none other than Officer Mario Lopez, one eyebrow raised in a look that screamed 'Seriously?'

He strolled up and rapped his knuckles on my window.

I rolled it down, giving him my best innocent grin.

"Morning, Mario," Landon said from the passenger side, shooting him a questioning look. "Everything okay?"

"Got a call about a domestic disturbance," Mario explained. "Apparently, there's been some shouting loud enough to scare the neighbors' cows." He jutted his chin toward the imposing manor looming behind us. "With Harold's recent passing, they were concerned and asked us to do a well check."

"We were just leaving, but Blanche seemed all right when we saw her," I offered. "It's her brother-in-law doing all the shouting. He's flown in from Las Vegas to claim everything his brother built. Or at least that's what it seemed like to me."

"Appreciate you letting me know. I'll go check on her." His hand rested casually on his holstered gun as he turned toward the house.

"Do we wait?" Landon asked quietly.

"Is that really a question?" I responded as we watched Mario head up the driveway toward the ongoing commotion.

"Fair point."

Suddenly more shouting erupted from the direction of the house.

"You called the cops, didn't you?" Anton's voice raged out. Even from here, we could hear the fury lacing his words. "Just to screw me out of what's mine!"

Blanche's voice rang out pleadingly in response. "No, Anton, I swear! Please, you have to calm down!"

Landon and I exchanged a wide-eyed look.

Mario picked up his pace, hand now gripping his weapon.

"Liar!" Anton roared, jabbing an accusing finger at her. "I know you want it all for yourself, you greedy, conniving—"

"That's enough!" Mario stepped between them, hands raised, placating. "Let's all just take a breath here."

"Do we go up there?" Landon whispered.

"Shhhhhhhh!" I told him.

"Stay out of this!" Anton yelled at Officer Lopez as if telling off a nosy neighbor rather than a cop just doing his job. "Is arguing against the law in this backward state? This is family business, and it's none of your business. So butt out!"

Anton took a menacing step toward Mario, who stood firm.

I winced, wondering if Anton was trying to get himself arrested.

Mouthing off at a police officer usually didn't end well.

"I don't know how it is in Las Vegas, but you really don't want to get in a police officer's face here in Texas," Mario said evenly, with the cool confidence of someone who knew they had authority on their side. Though his tone was calm, his fingertips tapped a staccato beat on the handle of his holstered gun like he was playing the drums to an intense rock song in his head.

"It'll be a lot of paperwork for me and a rough night involving some intimate time with a jail cell for you," he continued. "To avoid all that, I'm going to ask you to lower your voice and step back. Please."

"Or what? You'll arrest me?" Anton barked out a harsh laugh. "I'd like to see you try." He took another menacing step, fists clenched.

Mario's hand moved and now hovered near his Taser. Tapping his gun while talking to Anton might have been a tough-guy posture or a bluff, but the sleek, silver Tazer-X1 capable of immobilizing obnoxious poker players with a pulsating jolt of non-lethal force?

That was no bluff.

"Anton, no!" Blanche cried, clutching his arm. "Please, don't do this!"

Anton seemed to realize he was testing fate by staring down the wrong end of a Taser. He stepped back with a few grumbled curses, though his face still looked ready to combust.

"As I said, I'm here because your shouting

concerned the neighbors." Mario's gaze flickered between Anton and Blanche, his stance primed. "Ma'am, are you all right?"

"She's fine," Anton snarled, taking a half-step in front of Blanche. "She's rich and doesn't have to deal with my brother anymore. Right, Blanche?"

He shot her a pointed look.

Mario took a measured step closer to Blanche. "Let the lady speak for herself, sir." Though his words were calm, tension thrummed through them.

"I'm okay," she said softly. Her eyes betrayed a glimmer of fear before she hid it away.

Mario studied her a moment longer, clearly unconvinced. But with Anton glaring daggers at him and no clear reason to suspect a crime was taking place, he had little choice but to let it go for now.

"All right, then." He tipped his hat. "If y'all need anything, I'm just a phone call away. I think for the neighbors' health, it may be best if you both go inside and try to keep any arguments down to a dull roar. I'll be down the road if needed, at least for a bit."

"Come on, Anton," Blanche said softly, tugging his arm lightly to guide him toward the house. That action, as random and innocuous as a pebble in a pond, somehow triggered Anton to go supernova.

His face turned roughly the same shade as a fire engine as he jerked his arm away from Blanche's gentle grasp. If cartoon steam was coming from his ears before, now full geysers were erupting. I could practically see the dial turn as his temper shot from *Livid* to *Dangerous Rage Monster*.

"Don't you DARE touch me!" Anton thundered, flecks of spittle flying. Blanche recoiled as if he'd transformed into the Incredible Hulk before her eyes.

Officer Lopez shifted his stance, fingers drifting toward his Taser.

Uh oh.

I almost felt bad for Anton.

Almost.

Before Mario could react, Anton pulled back and swung a wild punch at the cop with all the coordination of a drunk ferret. Officer Lopez swiftly dodged the blow and then, reacting on instinct and muscle memory, whipped Anton around and slammed him face down onto the grass faster than you can say "police brutality lawsuit."

I winced as Anton hit the dirt hard, certain he'd have a mouthful of sod later.

So much for keeping things civilized.

"You're under arrest for assaulting an officer," Mario said gruffly, hauling Anton to his feet. Mario pulled out a pair of handcuffs, the metal clinking ominously. "You have the right to remain silent..." he recited as he wrenched Anton's hands behind his back.

As Mario dragged Anton past the driveway, the man's wild gaze suddenly landed on us. His lip curled in a sneer as he stared daggers at each of us in turn.

"You two!" he spat, struggling violently against

Mario's iron grip. "You called the police, didn't you? Nosy small town idiots!"

I instinctively shrank against Landon as Anton's venomous words washed over us. Landon's arm came around me, steady and protective.

"That's enough out of you," Mario said gruffly, giving Anton a shake. "Now pipe down and get in the car."

Anton twisted to glare at us a moment more, his expression promising unfinished business. "You'll regret this," he spat venomously before Mario shoved him into the waiting patrol car.

As Mario slammed the door shut, Blanche fled back into her house.

"So... breakfast tacos?" Landon asked me.

Chapter Eight

As tempting as breakfast tacos were, I couldn't bring myself to leave without checking on Blanche first. So despite Landon's grumbling stomach (which sounded like an angry bear coming out of hibernation), we walked back up the porch steps, and I knocked firmly on the imposing door.

After a few long moments, it creaked open.

Blanche stood before us, somehow looking even more fragile than before. Dark circles under her eyes stood out starkly against her pale skin. Her slim shoulders slumped with exhaustion beneath the weight of recent events.

"Oh, you're back," she said, managing a faint smile as we approached.

"We never left. We just wanted to make sure you're okay before we go. Do you need anything?"

Blanche tried to summon a brave smile, but it faltered. She blinked back tears, shaking her head. "Thank you for coming to check on me. After everything that just happened..." She trailed off, shaking her head.

"Of course. Like I said, we wanted to make sure you're okay," I said gently.

Blanche sighed. It was a weary sound that seemed to drain what little energy she had left. "I'm as okay as I can be, I suppose." She stepped back, gesturing us inside. "I'm sorry I didn't invite you in before. I just...with Anton's mood..." Her voice trailed off as she led us to the lavish sitting room.

"We understand," Landon said.

We settled onto an ornate sofa that looked like it belonged in a stuffy museum. I felt like I needed to sit perfectly upright and not touch anything. Blanche perched on the edge of an antique wingback chair like a bird ready to take flight.

"It's funny," she said after a moment, "Harold was never passionate or quick to anger. It's like Anton somehow got all those intense feelings that my husband lacked."

"Oh?" I was a little afraid to say more. Blanche looked one stray feather away from a total meltdown.

Her gaze grew distant, and her shoulders curled.

Landon and I exchanged a worried look.

"Is there anything we can do?" I asked. Again.

Why do people ask that over and over again in situations like this? It was like a reflexive response drilled into me despite it being about as useful as asking someone drowning if they've considered not sinking underwater.

"No. I'm so sorry you both had to witness that awful scene," she said. "Ever since Anton arrived, it's been nonstop drama. He's become like a madman obsessed with getting his hands on Harold's business and the investment money he swears Harold owes him."

"He certainly seems very fixated on it," Landon agreed. "If you don't mind my asking, what, exactly, is he claiming Harold promised him?"

Blanche sighed, her delicate shoulders rising and falling. "They were planning to go into business together selling NFTs of Harold's rare coins." Seeing my puzzled frown, she added, "Releasing digital versions for collectors to purchase online."

"I've heard of NFTs on the news, but I'm not very familiar with what they are," I said, scratching my head in that clueless way that always made Evie chuckle. I could feel my eyebrows scrunching together like confused caterpillars. "I think they have something to do with computers?"

"It stands for non-fungible tokens," Landon said as if explaining quantum physics to a golden retriever puppy. "Basically, digital assets stored on a blockchain that are bought and sold using cryptocurrency."

"Oh, right, of course," I said, nodding along like one of those bobblehead dolls. In reality, his explanation sounded like an alien language to me. Computer technology and I went together about as well as pickles and ice cream. Or Belladonna and dogs. But I didn't want to seem totally dense.

"The blockchain, got it," I added confidently.

Landon's lips twitched in a hint of an amused smile.

"I don't understand it all myself. But Harold was excited about reaching new collectors online while protecting his precious coins." Her smile faded. "Not that it matters now."

"Well, apparently, it matters to Anton," I said.

Blanche let out a brittle laugh. "The only thing that matters to Anton is what affects him. I don't know if I believe what he said. Anything he said, really. Harold never mentioned it, and the man could barely use a computer beyond looking up coin prices. Mabel handled all the cataloging and online listings for the store."

"You think he's trying to take advantage of the situation?" Landon asked.

She absently pleated the handkerchief between her fingers. "According to Anton, Harold promised to invest substantial sums toward this shared business venture. But Harold never said a word about investing in it to me."

Landon leaned forward. "Have you asked Mabel about it?"

"No, I..." Blanche hesitated, doubt flickering across her face. "Although I suppose it's possible she knew about it, and he just hadn't told me yet." She set the handkerchief aside and twisted a diamond tennis bracelet around her slender wrist instead. "To be perfectly honest, Harold didn't confide much to me about the shop's operations. Mabel handled the day-to-day affairs. So I can't say whether she and Anton were in contact regarding this NFT business."

I reached over and gave her hand a supportive squeeze.

"If you're not up to talking to Mabel, we could go speak with her about the NFT business," I offered gently, trying not to sound too eager.

Blanche dabbed at her eyes with a lace handkerchief, hand trembling. "Could you, Ellie? Honestly, after this whole fiasco with Anton, I just want to crawl into bed and pull the covers over my head for a while." She met my gaze. "But I'd like to know for sure one way or another from someone besides Anton. I just...I don't trust him."

My excitement at the investigative opportunity soured into guilt. Here I was, using Blanche's grief to feed my own nosy curiosity.

I was like a vulture circling roadkill.

Pushing back the icky manipulation I felt, I patted her hand. "Of course. You get some rest. Landon and I will talk to Mabel this afternoon."

Blanche managed a watery but grateful smile. As we left, I glanced back to see her sink into the wingback chair looking utterly spent. Like all the life force had been sucked out of her after surviving Hurricane Anton.

After leaving Blanche to rest and hopefully binge some comfort TV, we headed straight for Goldfinch Coins, tires crunching on gravel as we pulled into the lot. The 'Closed' sign still hung on the door, but when I tried the handle, it turned easily.

Exchanging a look with Landon, I pushed inside.

As we walked in, I half expected to hear a spooky "Hellllooo?" echo through the empty shop as dust moats swirled around us. The place reminded me of one of those ghost town stores in old Westerns, just waiting for a tumbleweed to blow by. All that was missing was the creaky swinging doors.

"Mabel?" I called softly.

A shuffling sound came from the back room, then Mabel appeared, blinking against the light. Her brown hair stuck out at odd angles like she'd stuck her finger in an electrical socket, and her eyes were bleary like she'd just woken from a nap at her desk or had one too many 'medicinal' gin and tonics.

"Oh, Ellie, Landon. Hi. I must have dozed off." She straightened her blouse, glancing around furtively despite the shop being empty. "You know I'm not supposed to be open yet. I don't even know if we'll ever open again. But I just had to get out of the house after..."

"No problem," I said cheerily, resisting the urge to whip out a feather duster and start cleaning. I lived with over a hundred cats and kept the dust bunnies lower than this coin shop.

"We understand," Landon said gently.

Mabel eyed us over her cat-eye glasses. "What are you two doing here?" she asked slowly, glancing between us like we might whip out handcuffs at any moment.

"We won't take up much of your time. We just had a couple of questions," I said with a faux casualness that sounded about as natural as a flamingo walking a dog. "Blanche sent us, actually. I think she's having a hard time, so she asked if we could talk with you."

It was abundantly clear we were here with some unspoken agenda and not a friendly visit, and Mabel's eyes narrowed further, glasses practically cutting into her face. At the mention of Blanche, though, she looked resigned to our questions. Her eyes darted around the dim shop. "Oh, well, I suppose..."

"Hey, Mabel? We know you're in a tough position," Landon said, taking another shot at convincing sincerity. "We just want to help take a little weight off Blanche's shoulders if we can, and she had some questions. But there's no pressure."

"I'll try to answer what I can. If I can." Mabel perched atop a nearby stool and waited.

Landon leaned against the display case, hands in his pockets. "Had you ever spoken with Harold's brother Anton before he showed up in town this week?" he asked.

Mabel tensed slightly. "Once or twice over the years,

on Harold's phone." She averted her eyes. "But we never met in person until the other day when he just appeared at the store."

I studied her carefully. "What was your impression of him from those calls?"

With a heavy sigh, Mabel removed her glasses and rubbed her eyes. "He could be very... intense. Even aggressive at times when making business demands of Harold." She shook her head. "He was nothing at all like mild-mannered Harold. I don't know how they were brothers, honestly."

"And you got all that from one or two phone calls?" Landon asked skeptically.

Mabel replaced her glasses with a trembling hand, her discomfort palpable as a porcupine in a balloon factory. She squirmed under Landon's questioning gaze like a worm on a hook.

"I, uh, well, I..." she stammered, eyes darting nervously.

It was obvious Mabel was hiding something juicier than a celebrity tell-all.

"Mabel, you said Anton was here the other day—don't you mean yesterday?"

She looked at me, puzzled. "No, Anton came by last Thursday. Harold seemed really surprised to see him just show up like that. They went in the back and got into a pretty heated argument."

I frowned. "But Harold was killed on Saturday. Blanche told us Anton arrived Sunday morning after catching a red eye from Vegas when he heard the news."

All color drained from Mabel's face. "Oh Lord," she gasped again, hand flying to cover her mouth. "You're absolutely right. I misspoke. Anton called on Thursday. He wasn't actually here." A nervous energy overtook her, and her words spilled out in a breathless rush. "I've just been so confused since Harold died. Very mixed up. I'm sorry, I meant Anton called Thursday. Just a phone call."

Landon and I exchanged a glance. "That seems like a pretty big mix-up to make."

Mabel's hands fluttered anxiously. "I know. I'm just so lost in grief and confusion right now." Her gaze darted between us. "Please forgive me for misspeaking. My mind is all muddled since Harold fell off the ladder."

I studied her carefully.

She seemed genuinely flustered, but was she covering for Anton?

Protecting his alibi?

Or, worse—was she covering for Blanche?

Did Blanche lie to us?

Lie to hide a conspiracy between her and that psycho brother?

I opened my mouth to press further when Landon caught my eye, giving an almost imperceptible shake of his head.

He was right—we didn't know the truth, so pushing Mabel now was pointless and would get the woman even more suspicious of our questions. I had a distinct feeling, though, truths were waiting to be uncovered in her stammering story.

I glanced toward the office at the rear. I saw a pillow and a rumpled blanket on the leather couch through the open door. Someone had been sleeping here.

I cleared my throat and turned back to Mabel. "We spoke with Anton Goldfinch earlier today."

Mabel's head jerked up, eyes rounding. "You did? Why?"

"He mentioned he and Harold were working on launching an NFT business together," I continued casually. "Selling digital coins for collectors. Do you know anything about that?"

Mabel nodded eagerly. "Oh yes, it would be ever so modern and high-tech. Harold was quite keen to step into the twenty-first century."

I frowned slightly.

That didn't align with what Blanche said about Harold's limited computer skills.

"So you and Anton were in contact about this business venture?" I pressed.

"Why yes, of course!" Mabel replied, but her pitch rose uncertainly. "I mean, naturally, I handled all of the particulars. Anton provided the, uh...the capital. I don't know the particular particulars, but I knew the *general* particulars."

She nodded firmly, but I noticed a sheen of sweat on her brow.

I noticed two things about her statement.

One? I had no idea you could use the word particular three times in one sentence.

Two? The details seemed hazy, and I couldn't help but notice that her account contradicted both Blanche and Anton's versions of events.

I shared another loaded look with Landon.

Mabel was clearly lying about something here.

Or Anton was.

Or Blanche was.

Or, heck, maybe everybody was.

Before I could inquire further, Mabel's cell phone rang. She glanced at it, and her eyes blew wide. "Oh dear, I have to take this!" she exclaimed breathlessly. "So sorry, but you really must be going now."

She practically pushed us out the front door with surprising force for her slight frame.

"Yes, bye-bye now! Best of luck with... whatever it is you're looking into!"

The door slammed shut behind us. Landon and I stood staring at each other.

"Well, that was..." I trailed off, at a loss.

"Weird and suspicious?" Landon supplied.

"Extremely."

We walked slowly back to the car.

Clearly, there was more connecting Mabel, Anton, and Harold. Mabel's jumpy, contradictory (and downright weird) account only deepened the mystery around Harold's death.

One thing was certain—Harold had either been keeping some major secrets from those closest to him, or he was the target of one whopper of a secret conspiracy.

Back at the shelter, I found Evie in the office and immediately launched into recounting everything that had transpired with Hurricane Anton, poor fragile (but possibly lying) Blanche, and shady Mabel. Evie's eyes narrowed thoughtfully as I described the shouting match at the Goldfinch estate and Mabel's cagey behavior at the coin shop.

"You're exaggerating," Evie said, looking at me incredulously.

"I wish I was. It really was that weird and wild," I said.

Evie shook her head in disbelief.

"I'm pretty sure Mabel is hiding something major at that coin shop," I added casually. "Or maybe about the coin shop? Nothing she said made sense, but since we don't know anything for sure, Landon felt it was better to back off and dig a bit."

Evie just blinked at me.

I didn't blame her—it was a lot to take in from one morning. With this crowd, we seemed to be one soap opera-worthy confrontation away from needing popcorn and comfy viewing seats to review everything that had happened on a gigantic whiteboard.

Evie made a beeline for her computer. "I might be able to dig something up on those two online," she said, cracking her knuckles. "NFTs are all about the digital space, right? But I'll need more specifics to effectively search. And I'm not sure how to get airline passenger lists to find out when the brother came in, but I'll try."

"We don't need them," Landon pointed out. "We can just go upstairs and ask Nugget. She was still at the shop on Thursday."

"Right. Okay." Evie fired off questions, fingers poised over the keyboard. "Full names?"

"Anton Goldfinch and Mabel Berry," I provided.

"Locations?"

"Well, Anton's from Vegas, although he flew in two days ago. And Mabel is local, obviously."

Evie's fingers flew as she typed. "Got it. Any usernames or online handles associated with them that you know of?"

How on earth would I know that?

I shook my head helplessly. "No idea, sorry."

"Hmm, okay. Don't need those to start." Evie squinted at the screen, scrutiny etched on her face. "Now let's see..."

For a couple minutes, she worked in silence apart from occasional murmurs to herself. I hovered nearby, impressed by her quick efficiency.

"Aha, here's something promising," she suddenly declared, swiveling the screen to face me and Landon. "I came across a thread on Interactopia referencing Harold's rare coin NFT project."

I leaned in eagerly.

The thread dated back over six months. Scanning the posts, I could see two users—VegasHighRoller and CoinQueen—discussing the launch of digital assets tied to Harold's collection.

"This is definitely Anton and Mabel; look." Evie turned the screen halfway back and scrolled through VegasHighRoller's posts on poker forums and subforums, stopping on a post where VegasHighRoller mentioned his brother, Harold, a coin collector. Then she pulled up CoinQueen's history of posts promoting Goldfinch Coins over the years.

"They aren't exactly subtle with their handles, and they talked about themselves in fairly identifiable ways," she said wryly. "This is them. No doubt."

"Nice work," I said, impressed. "So they were clearly both involved in this NFT project of Harold's."

Evie scrolled back through the posts, scrutinizing details. "Right, but the timeline they lay out here doesn't match up with what either of them told you guys today. If you recounted it right, I mean."

Rude.

She pointed out discrepancies—planned launch dates that didn't align and contradictory statements about who spearheaded certain aspects. In short, Harold Goldfinch was barely mentioned in the discussions at all, and Anton and Mabel seem to be taking primary responsibility for the project. The two of them, and one more person going by the handle "QuickdrawCounsel."

"Could QuickdrawCounsel be Harold?" I asked.

"No." Evie's pointed to the screen. "Look at this post. He said he's a lawyer." She clicked through QuickdrawCounsel and CoinQueen's Interactopia history, digging for insights. "Hmm, Mabel was ramping up promotion for this NFT project the last couple of months, talking it up all over..."

Suddenly she paused, squinting. "Well, that's odd."

Landon leaned closer. "What is?"

"This post from a week before Harold's death." Evie jabbed a finger at the screen. "Mabel essentially announced that the NFT launch was being postponed indefinitely. She implied it was due to Harold pulling the plug on the whole thing."

I re-read the post's frustrated tone. "And yet, according to Anton and his shouty screaming temper tantrum this morning, he and Harold were full steam ahead on the project when Harold died. And Mabel didn't mention anything about it being canceled to us."

"You sure?" Evie asked me.

"I'm not quite ready for the old folks home yet. Yes, I'm sure."

"Okay," she said and then shook her head. "I don't know." She pushed back from the desk, meeting my gaze. "I guess something pivotal happened right before Harold's death, some rift between him and his brother—or maybe Mabel tried to make it seem like a rift. I don't know. It's a lot of information, but nothing super-concrete."

She was right. There was a lot of info.

And nothing was definitive.

If we were hoping for an overly-dramatic, movie villain-esque post from an edgy username like 'Reaper666' claiming responsibility for Harold's death, we didn't find it.

Chapter Nine

I HELD THE DOOR OF THE ISOLATION ROOM OPEN, allowing Landon to enter first. Josephine was already inside, perched primly on a metal stool with a proprietary air about her. As we walked in, she arched one sharply sculpted eyebrow.

"Well, well. The intrepid investigators finally grace me with their presence. To what do I owe the honor?" Her words dripped sarcasm.

I frowned. "I don't understand what you mean."

Josephine speared us with an icy glare. "No? You two have decided to play detective with what could very well be a homicide investigation, interviewing witnesses and persons of interest willy-nilly. And you didn't think to inform me—an actual lawyer?"

"Now, hold on," Landon began, but Josephine silenced him with a slicing motion of her hand.

"Don't 'now hold on' me, mister. Do you have any

idea how unethical it is to conduct unofficial interrogations of possible suspects and witnesses? Not to mention the legal liability if you inadvertently obstructed justice or contaminated evidence?"

"We were just trying to gather some background for the police if it did turn out Harold was murdered. I swear we haven't contaminated anything." I shot her my most contrite, heartfelt gaze.

She harrumphed, unmoved. "I know we've developed a habit of playing Sherlock whenever someone gets their nose out of whack in this town, but you can't just barrel through without knowing the law. And you don't —I do. It's the lawyer thing. They made me go to school for that, you know. I have a license and everything, believe it or not."

"Who told you what we were doing?" I asked.

"Laurie, obviously."

Snitch.

"We understand your point, and you're right. We should have called you," Landon said soothingly. "You'll be happy to know we didn't find anything concrete anyway."

I nodded in agreement. "Right, we still have no idea if Harold was even murdered. Just that things are... complicated with the Goldfinches. Especially the brother, Anton—"

At the first mention of Anton Goldfinch, Nugget let out an ear-piercing yowl from her perch atop a nearby cat tree.

We all turned to look at her.

The petite tricolor was puffed up to three times her normal size, her back arched and fur standing on end. Her wide eyes were fixed on me, pupils dilated in fear. She shrieked again, sounding like a stepped-on squeaky toy, then took off at a full-tilt run. She streaked across the room and disappeared under a cabinet, still wailing piteously.

We all stared after her in shock.

"What was that about?" Josephine asked, bewildered.

I shook my head helplessly. "I have no idea. She seemed perfectly fine a minute ago."

"Strange," Landon murmured.

Josephine stood and crossed to the cabinet. She bent down, trying to coax the trembling tabby out of her hiding spot.

"Come here, darling. It's all right," she cooed in a gentle tone I wouldn't have thought the prickly woman capable of. "Why don't you jump on the disco plate and tell us what's bothering you, sweetums?"

Nugget refused to budge, growling low in her throat.

Josephine straightened with a sigh and turned back to us. "Any thoughts on what spooked her so badly?"

Landon's eyes narrowed thoughtfully. "I think it's pretty obvious that she understood what Ellie said, and that set her off." He hesitated, then continued, "She was about to tell you Anton Goldfinch seemed rather aggressive and antagonistic."

At the sound of Anton's name, Nugget unleashed another glass-shattering shriek. She scrabbled further under the cabinet as if trying to claw straight through the floor.

I stared at Landon. "She's absolutely terrified of Anton Goldfinch."

He nodded grimly. "For whatever reason, just the sound of his name sends her into a total panic."

Josephine's shrewd gaze bounced between us. "And how exactly do you two know Anton Goldfinch, anyway? Isn't he that poker-playing brother that had the run of bad luck in Las Vegas?"

I gave her a brief rundown of our encounters with Anton and his fiery clash with Blanche. Josephine looked thoughtful as she listened.

"I see," she said slowly when I finished. "I'd heard he was a piece of work."

"From who?"

"Blanche's friend Carla." Josephine tapped one slender finger against her chin. "We have an appointment to get our nails done at the same time each week, and she's shared quite a bit of gossip about the Goldfinches." Josephine glared. "Another reason you should have called me. Anyway, the question is—why?"

I blinked, confused. "Why what?"

"What transpired with Nugget and Anton to elicit such an intense reaction?"

Oh.

We're back on that.

"Excellent question," Landon replied. He turned his gaze on me. "I think we need to pay a visit to the police station. See if we can get Anton alone this time for a chat."

"I'm coming too," Josephine announced briskly, already grabbing her purse.

I blinked in surprise. "Why?"

She turned to me, one eyebrow raised imperiously. "You do remember I'm a lawyer, right?"

I wondered if Josephine's prestigious law degree was rolled up and hung on her wall like a baseball bat. It would certainly be appropriate, considering how often she figuratively whipped it out and hit us over the head with it.

A simple "trust me, I'm a lawyer" would suffice occasionally.

"Yes, Jo, I remember."

"You'll need someone with legal expertise if you're going to interrogate a murder suspect." She slipped on a blazer, straightening the lapels. "I can also help get you inside. They don't just let anyone stroll into the jail."

The small Tablerock police station was in an uproar when Landon and I arrived. Even from outside, the sounds of angry shouting and commotion seemed loud enough to rattle the windows.

Landon shot me a wary look as we approached the front doors. "Think Anton's still causing trouble?"

"I'd bet money on it," I sighed.

Sure enough, as soon as we entered the station, the source of the racket became abundantly clear.

"This is unconstitutional! I know my rights!" Anton Goldfinch bellowed from somewhere beyond the bullpen. "You can't hold me here like some common criminal!"

At the front desk, Mario had his head cradled in his hands. He looked up with an expression like a man who'd gone three rounds with a prize fighter as we approached.

"How long has Hurricane Anton been at that?" I asked.

Mario sighed. "I don't think the man even pauses to breathe."

A string of inventive curses flowed from the direction of the holding cells, creative enough to make a sailor blush.

"Has he managed to bully a lawyer into helping him yet?" Landon asked.

Mario shook his head wearily. "He refuses to call anyone local. Insists all Texas attorneys are incompetent hicks. Says he wants his own lawyers from Vegas flown in."

"Of course he does." I rolled my eyes.

"The guy definitely loves the sound of his own voice," Landon remarked as Anton launched into another tirade of shouted demands and complaints at full volume.

Mario pressed his fingertips to his temples. "You can say that again. I wish he came with a mute button. Or at least volume control."

The front door suddenly swung open, admitting a disheveled, perspiration-soaked man clutching a battered briefcase. His rumpled suit looked slept-in, his thinning hair stuck out at odd angles, and his eyes held a twister survivor's glazed, shell-shocked look.

"I'm here for Anton Goldfinch," he announced without preamble.

Mario arched an eyebrow. "You are?"

"Yes. I'm Ross Massey. I'm Mr. Goldfinch's attorney." He extracted a business card from his jacket and held it out.

Landon and I exchanged startled looks, both instantly recognizing the man. Slicked back hair, restless prowl—this was the same shifty figure we had observed in Harold's parking lot days ago. His edgy demeanor had caught our attention then.

Wasn't Massey Harold's lawyer, not Anton's? Why was Harold's business lawyer now representing his brother in a criminal arrest instead of, say, his widow in working out the transfer of Harold's business? And why was he in the parking lot outside the crime scene?

Mario studied the man's business card, then handed it back with a skeptical look. "Mr. Goldfinch claims he doesn't want any local lawyers. Says he's waiting for his team from Vegas."

Massey raked a hand through his hair. "Is that so? I think you're misinformed, Officer Lopez. When someone calls me ranting about police brutality and false arrest, I think it prudent to offer my assistance."

"How charitable of you," I muttered under my breath.

Ross Massey either didn't hear me or pretended not to. "May I see my client now?" he asked Mario impatiently.

"Yeah, all right." Mario led Ross toward the holding area, skepticism still etched on his face.

He paused before the doors, pointing a stern finger at Landon and me. "You two wait here." Then he and Ross disappeared inside.

I turned to Landon with raised eyebrows. "Am I crazy, or does this seem weird? That's the guy from outside Harold's store, right?"

"You're not crazy. It's definitely him, and it's definitely odd." Landon crossed his arms, frowning after where Ross and Mario had gone. "Wonder what Anton has over him to make that lawyer come running."

Before I could speculate, the front doors swung open again—this time admitting our friend Josephine Reynolds, clad in one of her customary smart pantsuits. Her gaze bounced between us in surprise. "Why, hello there. Fancy running into you two."

I quickly explained the situation with Anton's

ongoing tirade and Ross Massey's unexpected legal assistance. Josephine listened intently, manicured nails tapping against her cheek.

"That is odd," she mused when I finished. Her shrewd gaze traveled between Landon and me. "Correct me if I'm wrong, but wasn't Mr. Massey Harold Goldfinch's business attorney?"

I nodded. "Exactly. That's what makes this so strange. Why is he swooping in to help Anton instead of the widow?"

Landon raised an eyebrow. "And who called him?"

"If anyone," I said. "Mario said he didn't call local lawyers. He could have been lying about being called."

Josephine's eyes narrowed, lips pursing. Her gaze took on a knowing gleam. "Maybe Mr. Massey desires to stay abreast of developments in Harold's case. The question is... why?"

Before we could speculate further, the doors opened again, and Mario reappeared—this time with a scowl that could curdle milk. Without a word, he stomped to his desk, snatched up his keys, and turned back around.

"Mario?" I called out. "Everything okay?"

He turned back, swiping a hand over his hair in agitation. "That snake Massey showed up with paperwork insisting we have to release Anton immediately. Something about lack of evidence for the assault charge." Mario practically spat the words, disgust etched on his face.

My eyebrows shot up. "What? But we all saw Anton take a swing at you!"

"I did not," Josephine said evenly. "But that would seem like a one way ticket to a cozy cell for multiple days."

"Yeah, well, apparently Massey found some loophole to get the charge dropped, or some judge that didn't read the charge. I have no idea." He slammed a fist into his open palm. "I never even talked to a prosecutor."

I saw fury brewing beneath Mario's professional restraint. His jaw clenched so tight I feared for the integrity of his molars.

"Where are you going now?" I asked.

Mario sighed. "I've got to pick up that Monterey Nugget coin from the evidence room. Massey demanded its immediate release to the Goldfinch family now that the case is officially closed. He's got papers for that, too."

"They can't do that," Josephine said confidently as if quoting an infallible law of the universe instead of her personal opinion.

I resisted the urge to laugh.

If there was one thing I'd learned about small towns is that powerful people can do quite a bit if no one is willing to stand up to them.

"You're preaching to the choir. But they can, and they did." Mario scrubbed a hand over his face. "With Harold's death ruled accidental and Anton free, we've technically got no grounds to keep holding it." He turned to go with another muttered curse. Over his shoulder, he added, "I have a feeling this Massey situation is even shadier than it looks."

"And it looks pretty shady," Josephine said.

The door slammed shut behind him, leaving Landon, Josephine, and I staring after Mario in troubled silence.

After a few moments, I turned to my companions. "Why is everyone so quick to brush Harold's death under the rug and move on? First the sheriff, now this lawyer getting Anton released..." I huffed out a frustrated breath. "Am I crazy, or does this whole thing stink worse than week-old fish?"

"It absolutely reeks of corruption and cover-up. Mark my words, there are dark, powerful forces at work here, and justice is the furthest thing from their sinister minds," Josephine proclaimed dramatically. She stopped pacing and faced us. "Or it just looks mildly questionable on the surface, but there's a totally reasonable explanation. One of the two."

"That's a helpful observation," Landon said wryly, clearly trying not to roll his eyes.

Josephine's brand of help was certainly unique.

My mind churned with unanswered questions as we drove back to the cat shelter in thoughtful silence. Who was suppressing the investigation into Harold's death, and why? What was Ross Massey's connection to

Anton? Why was he at the crime scene? And what would it take to get real, transparent answers?

I shook my head, forcing the swirling thoughts away for now.

"I think I need a break. Just for a few hours, at least until Josephine gets back from the courthouse, and we figure out how Ross Massey pulled off what he did." As we pulled into the parking lot, I turned to Landon with a weary but genuine smile. "Want to help me clean the penthouse?"

His smiled. "Sure."

The "penthouse" was the mansion's third floor, a private area designed just for cats and not open to the public. With Landon's help, we'd created an oasis full of sunny windows, cozy cubbies, cat trees, scratching posts, and overstuffed cushions everywhere you looked in the large space.

It was a feline paradise, giving the rescues ample room to play, lounge, and relax away from humans.

My smile grew as we stepped inside, greeted by a chorus of welcoming meows and chirps. A fluffy Persian immediately trotted over to twine around my ankles while several tabbies peered down at us from their perches atop a towering cat tree.

Landon chuckled, bending to scratch a pair of tuxedo cats vying for his attention. "I think the penthouse residents are happy to have company."

"It's more than that, you know. They like you," I told him.

I began refreshing water bowls and scooping litter boxes, my worries fading as I lost myself in the simple, familiar tasks. It was hard to dwell on convoluted conspiracies with my scoopers full of actual cat poop.

We worked in comfortable silence for a while, the cats playfully weaving around our feet as we cleaned, until eventually, Landon spoke up as we cleaned nose prints from the windows. "So... you never answered my question yesterday. Not really."

"I didn't?" I paused in wiping down the window, crumpled newspaper dripping in my hand, and squinted against the streaky smudges left behind by our home-made vinegar cleaner. "What question was that?"

He moved to the next window, keeping his gaze focused on his task. "About us. I asked if you were doing okay with things between us. You asked what else it could be, which was kind of an answer—but I didn't feel like I really got a definitive answer out of you about us. How you feel about us. How you're doing with us."

"Oh, right." I suddenly became very interested in a smudge on the glass, studying it intently like it held the universe's secrets. Why hadn't I given Landon a straight answer yesterday instead of awkwardly deflecting? Didn't I answer? I'm sure I did. "Yep. I remember that conversation."

"And?" Landon prompted.

"I thought I did. Answer you."

"I'm sure you responded," he said, not letting me off the hook. "I'm not sure you answered."

I sighed internally. That man was like a dog with a bone sometimes. Or maybe a seasoned detective grilling an unwilling suspect. Once he latched onto something, good luck getting him to drop it before extracting what he wanted.

Taking a deep breath, I turned to face him.

"Things are wonderful between us, Landon. You make me happier than I've been in a very long time," I said, frantically trying to compose a response that would satisfy his persistence. Finally, I just opted to go with the truth. "Talking about it out loud just seems unnecessary, I guess. And a little scary sometimes."

Landon studied me for a moment, forehead creased in thought. "Because of how things ended with Evie's father?" he asked gently.

I froze, a lump forming in my throat.

I didn't want to talk about this.

He'd pushed too far.

"I don't want you to get offended by this, but I'm not ready to talk about this with you. In the interest of honesty, let's just say I never want to be that vulnerable again and leave it at that for now. Maybe someday I'll go more in depth about it, but not today."

Strong, warm arms enveloped me. I sank into Landon's embrace, comforted by his steadiness. "I'm sorry. I didn't mean to push. But, Ellie, I'm not him," he murmured against my hair. "I would never hurt you like that." His voice trailed off into pained silence.

"I know," I told him.

I wasn't entirely sure it was the truth... but I wanted it to be.

It's just that no one ever intends to hurt someone like that.

They just... do. Sometimes.

Landon leaned back to gaze into my eyes, his own glistening with emotion. "I'm not going anywhere." His hands framed my face, touch infinitely gentle. "I love you, Ellie. And I'll spend every day proving it if that's what it takes to help heal your heart."

Oh, dear Lord, why did he say that?

I drew a shuddering breath. "I love you, too."

Oh, dear Lord in Heaven, why did I say that?

The kiss we shared steadied my shaking, and when we finally pulled apart, Landon smiled at me tenderly. "So, can we make things official now?" His eyes shone with happiness. "Because I would really like to call you my girlfriend, and I would like to hear you not call me just a 'friend.'"

"You're such a teenager. But okay."

A chorus of impatient meows interrupted our moment. We turned to see over a dozen pairs of eyes watching us from around the room, tails twitching indignantly.

"How rude of us to stop petting them during all this mushy stuff," Landon chuckled.

Chapter Ten

THE CHEERFUL JINGLE OF THE SHELTER DOOR opening announced Josephine's return from the courthouse. Heads turned as she strode in, impeccably businesslike in a slim-fitting pantsuit and heels that clacked authoritatively on the tile floors. With brisk efficiency, her gaze zeroed in on the small table tucked away behind the reception desk where Landon and I waited.

Josephine settled into the chair, regarding us with an imperious eyebrow raise. "Well, you two certainly know how to find trouble."

I slid a wrapped sandwich and bottled tea across to her. "We also know how to find sandwiches," I said lightly.

Her stern expression softened slightly as she took a hearty bite, chewing with relish. After swallowing, she dabbed her mouth with a napkin. "That's actually pretty good."

"It's from Garcia's Market. So, what did you find out?" I asked.

Josephine's gaze hardened. "That Ross Massey is a contemptible, unscrupulous snake of a lawyer who knows how to manipulate the system to his own ends."

I shrugged. "I feel like we knew that when he showed up to get Anton."

"Well, now we've confirmed it."

"Confirmed what?" Landon's eyebrows shot up. "What exactly did you uncover at the courthouse?"

"Oh, it was masterfully executed, I must say. Despicable, but brilliantly so." Josephine dabbed at her mouth with a napkin, a glint of grudging appreciation in her eyes. "That man went before county Judge Horace Higgins, who only serves part-time when another judge calls in sick or goes on vacation and there's no one else to cover. Because he's a last resort."

I nodded, recalling the elderly, cantankerous judge's reputation.

Judge Horace Higgins was well past retirement age but stubbornly refused to fully relinquish the bench. These days he filled in only sporadically, grousing all the while about newfangled courtroom gadgets and young whippersnapper lawyers reading off their tablets.

"Back in my day, we had the law memorized in our heads and filed our briefs on paper, not these blasted screens!" he'd shout, brandishing a wavering finger.

The newer judges quietly endured his cantankerous lectures, knowing that despite his outdated views, rampant misogyny, and possible corruption, Horace would sit on any bench at any time. It ensured the regular judges could take vacations and days off whenever they liked, no matter what was happening in their courtroom—and it let them dump cases they didn't want to deal with on Judge Higgins.

"Now Judge Higgins and Massey go way back. They were part of the same good old boys golf and grill fraternity back when Massey was a young upstart fresh out of law school." Josephine leaned forward, lowering her voice conspiratorially. "And it just so happens that Judge Higgins recently came into enough money to buy himself a swanky new condo in Galveston with stunning gulf views."

"Maybe he has investments," Landon suggested.

Josephine shook her head. "His pension and social security. His wife stayed home to raise the kids and never worked a paying job a day."

My eyes widened as her implication sank in. "You really think Massey bribed the judge to secure Anton's release."

"Or Anton did, and Massey was the go-between. I can't prove anything other than suspicious timing and unaccounted-for cash." Josephine took another bite of her sandwich, looking pleased with herself.

"He can't just buy his way out of an assault charge," Landon said, incensed.

"Oh no? Where have you been living? You can buy your way out of anything with enough money."

Josephine waved her free hand airily. "Ethical and legal are hardly synonymous, darling. As far as I could tell, Massey executed everything by the book on paper. But I'd bet my law license some mighty shady dealings are lurking beneath the surface."

My gaze turned thoughtful. "What's in it for Massey?"

"That's a good question. Men like Massey don't risk their careers out of charity. There must be something else." Josephine stared into the distance, lips pursed. "Something big he has to gain."

I shook my head, just as perplexed. "Whatever his motive, it seems like too much effort just to do a favor for his dead client's obnoxious brother."

Landon crossed his arms over his broad chest. "Maybe the payoff comes later," he suggested. "Could Massey be angling for a cut of Harold's estate once the dust settles? Is there some way that could happen?"

"With no will, Blanche stands to inherit everything as Harold's wife. This is Texas—married people are essentially one person in this state." Josephine tapped a manicured nail against her chin. "Still, if Massey helped Anton secure a portion of the assets, he would likely demand a percentage."

"Do you think we should talk to Blanche again?" I asked. "Maybe she knows more about what Ross and Anton might be scheming. Or maybe she doesn't know they're scheming, and we need to tell her."

"It couldn't hurt," Landon agreed. "Although the

poor woman seemed overwhelmed enough with everything going on. I'd hate to bother her if we don't have to."

Josephine waved off his concern. "Oh, bother away. Forewarned is forearmed, as I always say. She needs to know what snakes are slithering in her midst."

I had to chuckle at Josephine's relentless enthusiasm for intrigue. "I guess we're paying Blanche another visit."

A jingle from the front door drew our attention. Darla (my shelter manager and Evie's best girlfriend) bustled in carrying a bakery box. "Ellie, I got the cookies for tonight's meet and greet event. Hello again, Ms. Reynolds! Did you want to try a cookie? I have ten more boxes in the car. I'm sure one couldn't hurt."

Josephine flashed her a smile. "I suppose one couldn't hurt."

As Darla handed Josephine a cookie, I frowned. "You know, I just realized something. When we saw Ross in the parking lot at Goldfinch Coins after Harold died, he looked like he'd been caught in a windstorm. All disheveled, with bags under his eyes like he hadn't slept."

Landon's eyes lit up with recollection. "You're right. He did look pretty haggard for a high-powered lawyer."

"Did I say he was high-powered?" Josephine asked. "I said he was a snake. You saw him at the crime scene?"

"Yes, in the parking lot outside. You know, he looked awful today, too."

"I'm not sure that means anything," Josephine said. She dusted a few stray crumbs from her fingers. "Ross

Massey is unscrupulous, and we can add hygienically challenged to the list. I'm less concerned with his showering habits and more concerned with why he was in the parking lot of his dead client's store." She looked at me. "Did you see him talk to the police? Harold was his client, after all."

I shook my head slowly. "No. I didn't see him talk to anybody." I frowned. "This whole thing just gets stranger and stranger."

Landon's expression mirrored my bewilderment. "No kidding"

"Murders are rarely straightforward." Josephine smiled slyly, holding her hand out toward Darla, who handed her another cookie. "Actually, I'm lying. They're usually straightforward. Just not in Tablerock, Texas, for some reason." She popped the cookie in her mouth.

Clutching some of the new cat toys delivered that morning, I hurried up the stairs toward the isolation room, eager to visit Nugget again.

Our last interaction still puzzled me. I was hoping with this new information about Anton, I might get some clarity on why she had reacted so strongly at the mention of his name.

Reaching the door, I paused. "Nugget?" I called softly as I eased inside.

Two perky ears popped up from behind a litter box,

followed by a pair of curious golden eyes. Nugget scampered over, weaving eagerly around my ankles. Kneeling down, I scratched under her chin as she purred loudly.

I stood up and stepped inside, closing the door behind me. Within seconds of the door closing, Belladonna leaped gracefully onto the glowing platter and fixed me with an imperious stare. "Well, well. Look who's come crawling back to beg my forgiveness after that appalling display of boorish behavior."

Nugget ran and hid in a cubby.

I blinked at Bella, momentarily confused. "Pardon me?"

"I've made myself perfectly clear."

Not as clear as she thinks, I thought. "Bella, what—"

"Are you going to distress the poor creature once more?"

Wow. I didn't think Belladonna gave much care for anyone other than herself. "Belladonna, I need to ask Nugget more about the Goldfinches. But I promise, I had no idea the mention of that man would—"

The black cat's coat practically exploded, puffing up so she looked like an insulted Gothic pom-pom. "Naturally, you've not come offering remorse, you reckless mortal. Gallivanting hither and yon, sowing chaos with nary a thought for whom your antics might afflict. Heedless, the lot of you!"

I took a deep breath, striving for patience. "Bella, I'm honestly quite happy to see you're protective of Nugget, and you're right—I should be more careful about triggering her anxiety. But there are questions I need to ask that could be important."

"Pah!" Belladonna spat. "Your endless interrogations are nothing more than self-serving drivel!"

From her cubby hole, Nugget peeked out, eyes wide as she took in the angry scene before her. After hesitating, her determination won out and she crept toward Belladonna. With a delicate step, she hopped up onto the crystal platter beside the dark feline menace.

As Nugget settled on the plate, its glow shifted and splintered, casting dazzling kaleidoscopes of color dancing around the room. "Please don't be upset because of me," Nugget said, her voice high and anxious. "I don't like it when everyone fights."

I gently scratched her head. "It's okay, sweetie. No one is fighting because of you." I shot Belladonna a pointed look.

The black cat sniffed in response. "Eleanor is right."

"See?" I told the calico.

"We're fighting because humans are idiots," Belladonna said.

Nugget seemed transfixed by the kaleidoscope of colors reflecting around the room. Tentatively, she stretched out a paw to bat at a nearby vibrant beam. "I'm sorry I got so scared about... him before," she said distractedly. "But he wasn't very nice to me or Master Harold."

I leaned in. "Nugget, can you tell me—did that not-nice man come to see Harold at the coin store before he... passed on?"

Nugget tilted her head. "Before he passed on? What does that mean?"

"On Thursday, maybe?"

"What's Thursday?"

Of course, asking a cat about specific days and dates was pointless. I'd have to rethink my approach.

"Did the mean man visit the coin store recently? Like, after the last time it rained, but before someone dropped you off here with us?" It had rained briefly last Tuesday, two days before Mabel had—at first—claimed Anton showed up at the store.

Nugget's nose crinkled as she considered this. After a moment, her eyes brightened with recognition. "Oh, you mean the loud time!" she exclaimed. "When the man was yelling and turned red. Yes, he came to see Harold then. Master Harold kept yelling that name and telling him to stop, but the man kept yelling back."

I felt bad, but I had to. "And the name was Anton?"

Nugget's ears flattened, and Belladonna and Nugget both hissed.

"Can I take that as a yes?"

"Yes," Nugget confirmed softly.

"Did you see or hear anything else when the loud man came?" I asked. "Or even anything this week at all. Anything that scared you or made you upset?"

Nugget scrunched up her face. "The other man with stinky fur that was smooth and shiny and crunchy."

A stinky man with too much hair product?

Had to be Ross Massey.

"Was his name Ross?" I asked. "Did you hear that name at all?"

Nugget cocked her head. "What's a Ross?"

Surely Nugget knew Harold's own business attorney? I made a mental note to get a picture of the lawyer and show it to Nugget later. "Never mind. It sounds like the mean man visited the coin store with Harold's lawyer, Ross Massey, right before Harold died."

"Oh! Mr. Massey? Yes. I know him." Nugget gave a somber nod.

I mulled over what Nugget had revealed. Harold and Massey had a long-standing business relationship, yet weren't close enough to be on a first-name basis. That detail spoke volumes. Their rapport was purely professional rather than friendly.

I stroked Nugget's back gently. "Thank you, sweetie. You've been a big help."

I stood to leave, meeting Belladonna's gaze. "I'm sorry our conversation got heated earlier. We don't have to agree, but I'll be more mindful of my future statements."

The black cat huffed in response, leaping down from the platter in a blur of black fur. But as I opened the door to exit, I could've sworn her second "Humph!" sounded slightly less contemptuous than usual.

I headed downstairs, my mind spinning with everything I'd learned from Nugget. Anton had been at the coin store right before Harold died, arguing with him over the rare Monterey Nugget coin. And he'd been there with Ross Massey, who clearly had some kind of shady business going on.

I found Evie in the back room, refilling treat jars. She glanced up with a smile. "Hey, Mom, Landon just popped over to his office to check on that cabinet job. He'll be back soon."

Before I could respond, Josephine entered the store room and cut in briskly. "Well? Did you discover anything useful from the cat?"

I peeked out the storeroom door and looked around. Once I was sure no one was nearby to overhear, I quickly relayed the details of my conversation with Nugget.

"Harold's brother Anton was there arguing with him within two days of his death. And even more interesting, Harold's lawyer, Ross Massey, might've been there too." I raised my eyebrows at Josephine.

"How very peculiar. A lawyer contracted in both sides of a brotherly squabble and winding up with two clients on opposite sides in the course of a week. One dead." Josephine tapped a manicured nail against her chin. "Highly irregular. More than a little suspect."

Evie looked back and forth between us. "So you think Anton or Ross could have killed Harold? But why? What's the motive?"

Josephine waved a hand airily. "Oh, who knows? Greed, resentment, a soured business deal—take your pick." She inspected her nails idly. "Although Ross's presence at the actual crime scene is awfully incriminating. I'd like to know how he explains that away."

"But we still have no idea who dropped off Nugget. We can't point fingers until we figure out who that woman is on the security footage, and we're clearly missing a huge part of the story."

Josephine nodded thoughtfully. "An excellent point, Evie. We're still missing a major piece of the puzzle. The very first piece, actually."

Just then, the front door opened again, and Landon hurried in.

"Success! My manager says they'll be done with the joisting by tomorrow," he announced triumphantly. Then he noticed our serious expressions. "Hey, did I miss something?"

"Only Ellie uncovering a veritable hive of lies and deception," Josephine said wryly. "Do keep up, darling."

Landon looked at me questioningly. I quickly summarized everything we'd learned from Nugget, and Evie repeated her observations.

"Huh." He scratched his head. "Well, it seems fishy that Anton and Massey were at the coin store in the days before Harold died. But Evie's right. We can't make any accusations without figuring out the mystery woman's role in all this."

I nodded. "We need more information before we can

start pointing fingers at anyone. We still don't even have a motive."

"Ben's murder was easier," Evie admitted. "Everyone had a motive."

"They're both effectively the same problem, and both are problems that need to be solved." Josephine checked the dainty gold watch on her wrist. "Well, duty calls. I'm expected back at the firm this afternoon. Do keep me updated if you uncover anything else juicy. Or if you wind up in jail."

With an airy wave, she sashayed out the door.

Chapter Eleven

The Silver Circle Cat Shelter bustled with activity as we put the finishing touches on preparations for the big mayoral candidates' *Meet and Greet* fundraiser I'd volunteered to host months before all this Harold Goldfinch business popped up. Volunteers scurried about hanging silver and blue streamers while I arranged trays of hors d'oeuvres.

"Having a party on a Monday evening? No one's going to come," Evie said as she blew by me with a plate of cookies. "Especially not since Harold died on Saturday."

"We made a commitment," I told her.

"Looking good, Ms. Rockwell!" Darla enthused as she bustled past us, her arms loaded with gift baskets for the raffle. "This event will be a huge success for Waldo's campaign—and for the Tablerock Women's Shelter."

"See?" I told my daughter. "Darla thinks it will be fine."

Evie rolled her eyes. "She's an optimist, even when it's unwarranted."

"I heard that!" Darla called back.

I sighed, knowing Evie had a point.

Still, with over a hundred attendees expected, the event would raise valuable awareness and funds to aid vulnerable women and children in our community. And, of course, with the mayoral election a couple of months away, it provided the perfect platform for the candidates to connect with voters.

I just hoped the presence of current Mayor Jessa Winthrop didn't stir up too much contention at this event. Her underhanded tactics, shady backroom deals, and general air of untrustworthiness had made her even more unpopular of late.

Which I didn't think was possible, given her popularity was already ranked somewhere between stubbing your toe and getting a root canal.

As six o'clock neared, guests began filtering into the event space, welcomed by the shelter's cheerful volunteers. I spotted many familiar faces from around town, including Officer Mario Lopez and Councilman Hammond. Dale Haberman, the owner of Dale's Donuts, arrived with the sleazy womanizer Dr. Canter. Joe and Zora Hillard came together, followed soon after by Josephine Reynolds, looking elegant as always. Even Blanche Goldfinch showed up, which seemed...

Odd.

It seemed odd.

I was chatting with Darla when Laurie bustled up to us, clad in a tasteful black sheath dress rather than her usual scrubs. "Ellie, everything is just lovely. You've outdone yourself," she said with a wink. Before I could respond, she gasped loudly, grabbing my arm. "Oh my word, is that who I think it is?"

I followed her scandalized gaze to see none other than Mabel Berry slipping quietly into the front room, looking around self-consciously. Her mousy brown hair was pulled back in a tight bun, and she wore the same owlish glasses as always. Her dress (in an unflattering shade of mauve) did little to improve her appearance.

"I'm starting to wonder what was really going on with the women in Harold's life that the two of them are ready to party forty-eight hours after he shuffled off this mortal coil," Laurie said under her breath. "I've had clients that mourned their dogs longer."

I shot her a look.

Mabel seemed harmless enough to me, if a bit odd—though I had to admit, her arrival was unexpected. I hadn't anticipated Harold Goldfinch's timid assistant feeling comfortable mingling at a social event so soon after his death—especially not with gossip swirling about her possible romantic feelings for her deceased employer (and considering she clearly knew something she wasn't saying).

Before I could dwell on it further, the candidates

themselves arrived—Mayor Jessa Winthrop first, followed soon after by her opponent, Waldo Monroe. As the guests gathered, I stepped up to the mic Evie'd installed at the front of the room to kick off the speeches and fundraising efforts. I kept my comments brief, emphasizing our shared duty to support the women's shelter, playing up the excitement at having two mayoral candidates for a change and wishing both Jessa and Waldo the best of luck in the election.

Waldo took the mic next, cutting an impressive figure in a crisp navy suit that showed off his athletic build. As a successful martial arts school owner, Waldo exuded an air of quiet confidence. He spoke passionately about his vision for improving life in Tablerock through smart economic policies and protecting green spaces. The sincerity in his voice was obvious.

Scattered applause broke out when he finished. I noticed Mabel studying him thoughtfully from her spot along the back wall, looking intrigued.

When Mayor Winthrop's turn came, she pasted on a syrupy smile that didn't reach her eyes and launched into a rambling speech full of ten-dollar words but little substance. Her gaze bounced around the room as she spoke, likely trying to gauge how her platitudes were being received by these influential voters.

I suppressed an eye roll and glanced around.

Many had polite, fixed smiles but otherwise seemed distracted, their attention drifting. More than a few had narrowed eyes or pursed lips, apparently seeing through the mayor's glossy veneer—much to her poorly concealed annoyance. As Jessa droned on, I noticed guests leaning close to whisper among themselves, no doubt trading commentary about her pretentious rhetoric.

Laurie sidled over to where Dale and I stood along the back of the room with crossed arms and bored expressions. "Think anyone is buying this nonsense besides her?" she muttered under her breath.

Dale stifled a snort. "Not likely. That woman couldn't sound more fake if she tried."

As the mayor's speech continued, I let my own gaze wander. Mabel still hovered near the back, shoulders hunched self-consciously. She appeared deep in thought, though she glanced up nervously when anyone drew near. Two nearby women were eyeing Mabel and whispering while pretending to listen to Jessa's ongoing drivel.

I edged closer to them, straining to catch what they were saying.

"It's downright tacky if you ask me," the first woman sniffed, loud enough to be sure Mabel overheard. "Showing up to rub shoulders after her boss kicks the bucket under such suspicious circumstances? And at the same party as his widow?"

Her companion nodded sagely. "No class at all. Mark my words; that mousy little spinster knows more than she's letting on about what really happened to Harold Goldfinch. Showing up where she knew

Blanche would be. It's a scandal, I tell you. That poor woman."

This town, I thought sourly.

Before I could decide whether or not to intervene, Jessa's speech ended with scattered, obligatory applause. Guests immediately began circulating again, separating into small clusters to chat and nibble hors d'oeuvres. I noticed Blanche accept a glass of wine from one of the volunteers before blending seamlessly into the networking crowd, her manners as polished as ever.

I wove among the various groups, smiling and chatting. When I reached Matt and Evie, their conversation paused abruptly. A guilty glance passed between them before Evie plastered on a bright smile.

"Great event so far, Mom! You really went all out," she said breathlessly.

Too breathlessly.

I smiled, deciding not to pry about whatever they'd whispered moments before. "Well, it's a great cause. I'm glad to see so many people turn out to show their support." I raised my glass. "Here's to Waldo unseating our esteemed mayor come November."

Evie and Matt clinked their glasses to mine, murmuring in agreement. As I sipped my sparkling cider, I noticed Landon across the room, deep in conversation with Mario Lopez and another man I didn't recognize. His arms were crossed, forehead creased in a thoughtful frown as Mario spoke.

Catching my eye, Landon tilted his head subtly

toward the doorway and then back at me, an unspoken signal. Message received. He wanted a private word away from the bustling crowd. I wound my way over as casually as possible while Landon extracted himself from the conversation.

We slipped into the empty hallway, and Landon's solemn expression sent a coil of unease through my stomach. "What's going on?" I asked. "Did something happen?"

"Maybe. Mario got a call from Don Markham. They finished reviewing footage from security cameras from the shopping center the day Harold died." His jaw tightened. "And it looks like several key minutes were deleted somehow. Right when someone would have been leaving the shop if they'd done Harold in."

My eyes widened. "What? But who could have—"

"Exactly," Landon cut in grimly. "Someone deleted that footage deliberately."

I exhaled slowly, thoughts swirling. "Then Harold's death definitely wasn't an accident. This proves it."

Landon nodded. "Prove it? No. Make Markham suspicious this wasn't an accident?" His expression hardened with determination. "Yep."

"Attention guests–the raffle drawing will begin in five minutes!" Darla's voice rang out over the chatter, instantly igniting a buzz of excitement among the crowd.

I glanced reluctantly back toward the front, where the festivities were still in full swing, lively voices and laughter spilling into the hall. The disturbing revelation Landon had shared cast a dark pall over the cheery event, but we had a roomful of expectant donors awaiting the gift basket raffle, and as the host, my presence was probably required.

With a weary sigh, I slipped my fundraiser smile back into place. "I guess that's my cue. We can talk more about this later."

Landon nodded, giving my shoulder a reassuring squeeze before rejoining the mingling guests. I wove through the clusters of people exchanging spirited small talk and good-natured debate about the candidates' messages, trying not to let my unease show.

Nearing the makeshift stage at the front of the room, I spotted Laurie deep in hushed conversation with Josephine and Blanche Goldfinch. With their voices barely above a whisper I had to strain to hear as I walked up.

"...and she pretends not to hear the vicious gossip, but I know it's wearing on her," Laurie said earnestly, with frequent glances toward the back of the room. I followed her gaze to see Mabel standing alone again, staring at her shoes.

Josephine shook her head, lips pursed in sympathy. "People can be so cruel."

"It's disgraceful," Blanche agreed, looking distressed. "That poor woman idolized Harold. Whatever she may or may not feel for him, she lost her dear friend and livelihood. These harpies delight in kicking someone when they're down."

Clearing my throat, I stepped up with a bright smile. "Don't let me interrupt. Just wanted to let you ladies know the raffle is starting."

They returned my smile, turning to find seats as cheerful chatter continued to fill the room. I made my way through the bustling crowd over to where Darla stood beaming near the makeshift stage. She eagerly thrust a large wicker basket into my arms, stacked high with gift certificates and assorted goodies we would be giving out to the winners.

Darla stepped up to the microphone, her smile bright.

"Thank you all again for being here tonight and supporting the Tablerock Women's Shelter," she began, waiting for the smattering of applause to fade. "And now, the moment you've been waiting for–it's time to draw the winning raffle tickets for our amazing prize baskets!"

I held up the first luxurious, overstuffed gift basket as Darla called out the winning ticket number. Gasps and enthusiastic cheers erupted from the crowd when Josephine Reynolds was announced as the winner. With a graceful smile, she glided up to collect her bounty.

"How lovely! A wonderful cause deserves wonderful gifts," she proclaimed as she breezed back to her seat, clutching the massive basket against her frame.

I drew ticket after ticket as Darla announced the winners for each of the incredible local business gift baskets I held up. As the stacks dwindled, a hush fell over the guests, every eye fixed intently on the remaining baskets. I knew what prize they were all hoping for–the scrumptious Sunday Sweets tower of treats donated by Augusta Walton, piled impossibly high with delectable baked goods and gourmet chocolates from her high-end bakery.

It was always the most coveted basket at any fundraiser.

Darla gave an impromptu drumroll on the podium, ratcheting up the anticipation. "And the winner of the incredible Sunday Sweets gift basket is..."

I slid my hand into the fishbowl and withdrew the final slip of paper. Unfolding it slowly, I read out, "Ticket number 63!"

An excited squeal rang out as Zora Hillard leaped to her feet, hands clasped to her chest in glee. "That's me. I won!" she cried, rushing forward to claim her sugary bounty like a miner who'd just struck gold. "I never win anything!"

I heard someone in the crowd poorly stifle a snort.

Zora didn't need to win anything—she was wealthier than a Swiss bank thanks to her family's commercial real estate empire.

Joe Hillard, her husband, cheered proudly from his seat as Zora continued fawning over the basket of baked goods en route back to her chair, nearly stumbling in her excitement.

Finally, only one basket remained–the book basket, overflowing with hardcovers, paperbacks, gift cards for the local bookstore, and fancy bookmarks. "And last but not least," Darla said as I held up the final basket, "winner of the amazing book basket is... ticket number 107!"

A stunned gasp came from the back of the room. I looked up to see Mabel blinking rapidly behind her oversized glasses, her hands worrying the fabric of her ill-fitting dress. "Oh my, did you say one hundred and seven?" she asked tremulously.

"That's right! You won the book basket. Come on up!" Darla said warmly.

Mabel stood frozen in shock for another moment before visibly gathering her courage. With small, awkward steps, she navigated her way up to the front, staring at the basket in disbelief as if she'd just been handed the keys to a luxury car rather than a humble assortment of books.

"I never win anything, either," she breathed, hugging the basket to her chest. "Thank you so much."

I smiled against my better judgment, oddly happy to see her win something after the callous gossip she'd endured all evening (even though she might, in fact, be a murderer). Mabel clutched her prize tightly as she slipped back through the dispersing crowd to her seat along the wall once more.

"Congratulations," Blanche said with a smile.

"Uh huh," Mabel told her.

I stepped up to the microphone for the final thanks and farewells.

As the last few guests filtered out, we sank onto chairs with weary sighs, relaxing at last after the busy event.

Josephine inspected a tiny scuff mark on her heels with a moue of distaste. "Well, that was...interesting, I suppose."

"That's one word for it," Laurie snorted, flexing her feet gingerly after hours spent keeping up pleasing chatter in three-inch heels. "I can't decide if these meet-and-greets are energizing or exhausting. My feet are screaming that it's the latter."

Evie nodded, absently massaging a crick in her neck. "I'm with you there. But it seemed like a success overall, right?" She glanced around for confirmation.

"Absolutely!" Darla enthused. "The donations were fantastic, and everyone had a great time." Her boundless pep remained unaffected by fatigue.

I managed a weary smile. "You're right, Darla. And raising awareness and funds for the women's shelter is what truly matters." I hesitated, debating how much to share about the new information Landon and I had learned.

Laurie's sharp gaze landed on me. "But that's not all you're thinking about, is it? Spill, Ellie."

With an internal sigh, I gave them a brief rundown of the deleted security footage. I expected shock or dismay, but my news was met with knowing glances exchanged.

"You already knew," I surmised.

Evie bit her lip. "Landon might have given us a heads up." At my exasperated look, she rushed to add, "Just the people in this room! We didn't spread it around, I swear."

I shook my head, too tired to muster any real annoyance. "It's all right." I frowned. "I can't believe someone went to such lengths to cover their tracks. Didn't they realize that would be suspicious?"

"It means Harold Goldfinch was murdered, plain and simple," Josephine declared. "And the guilty party is still walking free somewhere in our idyllic community."

"Idyllic community?" Laurie asked, eyes wide in disbelief. "What town do you live in, again? Because it isn't Tablerock."

Landon walked up and leaned forward, jumping into the conversation as if he'd been there all along. "Here's what I can't figure out. Why was Harold killed? Was it money or business gain? Was he cheating on Blanche? Is it some DaVinci Code-like conspiracy? We're no closer to narrowing down a possible motive." His frown deepened. "What aren't we seeing?"

Darla's brow furrowed. "Do you think one of

tonight's guests could be the killer?" Her wide eyes bounced between us anxiously.

"Well, obviously, it's very possible," Josephine said.

Darla paled.

"Now, Josie, let's not panic anyone unnecessarily," I told her. "We have no actual evidence to suspect anyone of anything."

"Gossip is always distasteful," Josephine said. "That's why it's entertaining."

Laurie waved a hand. "We all know how people in this town love to wag their tongues regardless of the truth." She leaned in, lowering her voice conspiratorially. "We could find out from a reliable source whether there was anything improper between Harold and Mabel."

My ears perked up at the implication. "A reliable source? Do tell."

"Nugget?" At my stunned look, Laurie laughed. "Just ask the cat if they ever snuggled up with one another. The cat lived at the shop. The cat would know if Mabel and Harold were getting it on."

Evie nodded slowly. "Yeah, that's true."

"It'll help us figure out where to focus," Laurie said. "Though I must say, her presence tonight struck me as odd. And then her weird vibe when she won that raffle..." She trailed off, looking thoughtful. "I don't know. She looked like she wanted to be anywhere but here. I don't understand why she showed up."

"I don't understand why Blanche showed up," Darla said, brow furrowed.

"She works for the campaign," I explained.

"Jessa's?" Josephine gasped. The lawyer looked scandalized.

"No, no—Waldo's," I clarified.

Josephine pressed a hand to her chest, visibly relieved. "That makes much more sense. Supporting that crook Jessa would be unconscionable."

"Back to the original subject," Landon said, crossing his arms pensively. "You know who I find suspicious? That slick lawyer, Ross Massey. He showed up at the crime scene, got Anton released..."

"Not Anton?" I cut in. "I mean, Anton's clearly a few fries short of a Happy Meal. He's got my vote for prime suspect."

Landon shook his head. "But he's so obvious. I feel like someone who committed a calculated crime like this would be more subtle, you know?"

I chuckled. "You need it to be complicated, don't you? A wild-eyed rage monster bluntly threatening people and hitting cops in broad daylight isn't convoluted enough? The culprit is probably exactly who you'd expect—the shoutiest, most temperamental person with a history of violence."

Evie's nose crinkled. "I don't know, Mom. Landon has a point."

"This isn't a spy movie, it's small town drama," Matt

said. "As for Ross and Harold, they worked together for years. Wouldn't it be risky to kill his own client?"

"Greed makes people do crazy things," Josephine remarked.

Twenty minutes later, having bid goodnight to the others, Landon and I sank into the sofa. My muscles ached, and fatigue clouded my thoughts. But nagging suspicions still swirled, preventing full relaxation.

Landon reached over, giving my hand a gentle squeeze. "That brilliant, relentless mind of yours is working overtime," he observed knowingly. "Penny for your thoughts?"

I smiled tiredly. "Just turning over everything we talked about tonight. My gut says the truth is right under our noses if we keep digging." I shook my head. "We're missing something big. I know it. But I don't know what."

"We'll figure it out," Landon said with calm assurance. "Whatever trouble is brewing, we'll get to the bottom of it. We always do."

I nodded, buoyed as always by his quiet confidence. If anyone could unravel this mystery, it was our unconventional team of sleuths.

One way or another, justice would be served.

Harold Goldfinch's killer was free on borrowed time.

I hoped.

Chapter Twelve

The morning sun filtering into my office cast a deceptively cheerful glow as I sipped coffee and tried in vain to focus on paperwork. No matter how firmly I redirected my wandering thoughts, unanswered questions about Harold Goldfinch persisted in nagging at the fringes of my mind.

Sighing, I set down my pen and leaned back in my chair, rubbing my temples. The past week's events played like a mental slideshow—Nugget's panicked arrival, the reveal of the priceless Monterey Nugget coin on our land, Anton's volatile presence, the missing security footage...

A soft rap at the open door drew my attention. Evie stood there, an apologetic smile on her face. "Sorry to bother you. Darla and I finished the supply inventory if you want to review it. Have you talked to Nugget yet?"

"Not yet. I invited Laurie and Josephine over for

lunch, and we'll all go talk to her then." I waved Evie over to the spare seat, gratefully abandoning the paperwork that was giving me a headache.

"Not Landon?"

"He's been getting behind and needs to catch up on that big order. I promised him I wouldn't do anything too crazy without him." As Evie handed me the clipboard, I asked, "How are you and Matt doing, by the way?"

"Matt and me?" My daughter's face lit up at the mention of her boyfriend. "He's so amazing. Like, crazy amazing. He's supposed to be coming by this morning after school." She checked the time on her phone. "Shoot. He should be on his way now, and I'm not done sweeping the penthouse. Anything else?"

I shook my head, my thoughts turning to the changes I'd noticed in Evie since she started dating Matt. She seemed to carry herself with more confidence now. Her smiles came easier, the laughter more freely. Evie practically glowed whenever Matt walked into the room.

"Mom?" she prodded.

"Sorry. No, go ahead, we're good."

Evie nodded and headed for the door. As she reached out, her blouse fell open, exposing the gruesome scar that marked the multiple times doctors had sliced into her chest to save her life. The raised, discolored tissue served as a permanent reminder of the countless times her weak heart had brought her to the brink, only to be pulled back by the desperate hands of surgeons.

A reminder of surgeons I was so grateful for and a

disease I hated, one that caused her immense amounts of anxiety...

Anxiety that appeared lessened now, I had to admit.

Panic attacks that once frequently overwhelmed her were now few and far between. In their place was a sense of calm and assurance—a transformation I never expected to see in my sensitive, insecure daughter.

Matt's steady, caring presence had drawn out a side of Evie I wasn't sure existed. He valued her for exactly who she was, and his unwavering belief in her (and them together) was contagious. Matt truly seemed to cherish Evie, and she flourished in that devotion.

The kids made romantic relationships and overcoming problems look easy. I chuckled.

My cell phone buzzed with an incoming call, and my pulse quickened to see Mario Lopez's name on the screen. "Oh, goodness, I wonder what's happened now," I murmured. Ducking into the small courtyard garden behind my office, I swiped to accept the call. "Mario, perfect timing. I was just thinking about—"

"Ellie." His grim tone cut me off. "We've got a situation."

I straightened, alarm prickling down my spine. "What is it? What's happened now?"

Mario sighed heavily. "Anton Goldfinch reported his brother's vintage Corvette stolen from the mansion's garage. But the gate and garage were still locked with no signs of forced entry. Whoever took it must have had a set of keys."

My eyes widened. I pictured the cherry-red vintage sports car Harold had cherished so much he rarely drove it. "Anton reported it stolen," I repeated. "But what does he have to do with Harold's cars? Wouldn't they be in Blanche's possession until a will was read?"

"If either of the Goldfinches had answers, I'd tell you." Mario's frustration was palpable. "But I was just at that house, and Blanche was nearly hysterical, insisting to the brother-in-law that she had no clue how this happened, apologizing... I don't know, like she owed him something. And Anton is on the warpath, as you can imagine. But here's the funny part—he demanded we arrest 'that conniving thief Massey' immediately. He had no question the lawyer took the car."

I blinked. "The lawyer? Ross Massey?"

"Anton seems to think so," Mario confirmed. "According to Anton's ranting tirade, Massey demanded Anton give him the Corvette as payment for services rendered."

Mario's account left me scratching my head in bafflement. "Wait, I'm confused. For services rendered to Harold or Anton?" I asked, my mind spinning as I tried to make sense of this puzzle.

"Your guess is as good as mine. He didn't want to clarify."

"What on earth is going on here, Mario?" I murmured, more thinking aloud than really asking. My mind whirled as I mentally sifted through the facts, trying to discern a pattern. "I don't understand any of this."

Mario grunted in agreement. "No idea. And we've still got zero evidence of anything beyond the standard family squabbles that happen around money when someone dies with it." I could envision Mario's scowl. "Meanwhile, I'm stuck dealing with Hurricane Anton and his nonstop threats."

"Any luck tracking down the mystery woman on our security footage yet?"

"Unfortunately, no," Mario said. "The tech team hasn't found any definitive matches in our databases. Whoever she is, she's done a good job covering her tracks so far. Though that just entailed not looking up and staring at the camera, so make of that whatever you want." His tone turned wry. "Let me guess—you and Landon are going to launch some amateur investigation into the stolen car?"

I chuckled. "Are we that predictable?"

"Like the sunrise." Mario's voice held an unmistakable note of affection beneath the teasing. "Just do me a favor and be careful. And if you find the car? Don't go near it. Don't touch it. The last thing I need is for you people to accidentally tamper with evidence or get yourselves arrested for trespassing."

"No promises," I told him. Mario knew his attempt to rein us in was like trying to contain enthusiastic but clumsy Labrador puppies—nearly impossible.

"You do remember I can arrest you people, right?"

We exchanged farewells, and I hung up feeling more confused than ever.

The late morning sun beat down in a cloudless blue sky, baking the rolling hills surrounding Wardwell Manor in warmth. As I headed out to the cat-friendly garden, a faded wicker basket lightly against my hip, the buzzing of bees and chirping of birds filled the air with a melodic hum.

A refreshing breeze ruffled the leaves overhead and caressed my skin, carrying the scent of our garden's fresh catnip. I gently ran my fingers over the soft, downy leaves, releasing more of their intoxicating minty fragrance before plucking them and placing them in my basket.

Humming tunelessly, I savored the tranquility of this perfect summer morning. With sunlight dappling through the trees and a light breeze keeping me company, it was a picture of peace and a welcome respite.

As I drew closer, the crunch of gravel under tires announced an arriving vehicle in the staff parking lot. I turned to see Laurie pulling up in her dusty car. In one swift motion, she opened the creaky door and slammed it shut with a metallic bang. Her eyes blazed with purpose as she strode toward me.

"You're here a little early for lunch," I observed.

Laurie dredged up the ghost of a smile. "Unfortunately. My brain refused to quiet down last night." She hesitated. "I was actually hoping we could talk privately."

I studied her face, noticing the dark circles under her eyes and the uncharacteristic somberness in her expression. "I can do the rest of this later on today or tomorrow. Come on back to my place, and I'll make us some tea."

Soon we were seated across from each other at my cozy kitchen table, mugs of fragrant chamomile tea steaming between us. Laurie wrapped her hands tightly around the heated ceramic of her cup, clinging to it like a lifeline.

I kept my tone gentle. "What's on your mind, Laurie?"

Laurie sighed heavily, looking down into her mug. "I wanted to check in with you about using the magical plate on animals—well, dogs—in the isolation room. I know that area is Belladonna's domain, and I don't want to overstep. I feel like I overstepped."

I blinked. "The arm she shred to ribbons?"

She met my gaze. "That, and Evie mentioned she seemed extra irritable lately, and I can't help but wonder if I'm causing unnecessary stress by bringing patients in there so often. I think maybe I've forgotten she's still a cat with all the territorial needs and temperamental issues they can have as a domesticated species. I don't want to disrupt the peace or make life harder for you and that temperamental furball."

I waved a hand dismissively. "I think Belladonna's probably always been a drama queen quick to take offense. Her moods are more unpredictable than a moody teenager." I smiled kindly. "I appreciate your concern, but you provide an invaluable service to the animals in Tablerock. I'm happy for the plate to be useful."

Laurie still looked uncertain, biting her lip. "Are you sure? Like I said, I know how territorial she can be, and I don't want to push my luck. Maybe I should cut back on using the room for now..."

"I think you need to talk to Belladonna about it and maybe renegotiate the boundaries of your agreement," I said. "I'd pay closer attention to how she's responding, and if she seems truly distressed, talk to her. But don't stop helping animals, Laurie. I don't want you to do that."

Laurie finally smiled, looking relieved. "You're right, of course. I know you're right. I appreciate you letting me use the space, and I'll try to respect Her Royal Majesty's boundaries." She paused. "If I can ever figure out what they are, anyway."

"Absurd. Preposterous. Utterly farcical." Josephine Reynolds stabbed a forkful of salad at a table in the cat café, punctuating each word with a sharp jab. "Only a fool would fail to recognize these events clearly point to foul play."

"Did you just call me a fool?" I asked.

"No. I called Mario a fool."

Across the table, Evie and I exchanged amused looks at the lawyer's dramatics. Josephine had been holding forth on the outlandish nature of Tablerock's recent troubles ever since we gathered for a quick lunch and update.

"Granted, it seems suspicious," I allowed. "But is Massey foolish enough to steal Harold's car right after his death?"

"I doubt he believes he stole it."

"What do you mean?"

"He's a lawyer, after all. He'll have some basis for his actions somewhere." Josephine delicately patted her lips with a napkin. "But as to the real crux of your question—my dear, men have committed far stupider crimes in the name of greed or passion." She took a dainty sip of iced tea, pinky raised. "Let's not forget that the vehicle vanished from a locked garage. That suggests an inside job—if it's even a theft. Someone with access to the estate likely just drove it off."

"What about Anton?" Evie asked. "He probably has keys if he keeps showing up at the house to bother Blanche, and we know he's got a temper. Maybe he hid the car to frame Massey or get him out of the way or something."

I nodded thoughtfully. "It seems like Anton's been

causing nonstop drama and making wild accusations since he set foot in our town—but I still don't understand what he would gain from something like that."

"The problem, dear Ellie, is that none of you know what is happening or what Anton is here to gain. I'm glad, by the way, you're not charging anyone for this investigative work," Josephine remarked archly. "Even a broken clock is right twice a day, and all that, but you people haven't turned up any evidence of anything. And that's with a talking cat that lived with the victim in your possession."

I glared at her. "You're a real charmer, you know that?"

"My husband tells me that all the time."

"Your husband lies."

The bell above the café door jingled, drawing our attention. Laurie bustled in, spotted us, and hurried over. "Sorry I'm late! Big emergency surgery on a Saint Bernard who swallowed an entire corn cob. Good thing I came in early this morning." She pulled out a chair with a sigh of relief. "Did I miss anything?"

"Only the usual intrigue, drama, and criminal misdeeds plaguing our once-peaceful town," Josephine said dryly, bringing Laurie up to speed between delicate bites of her Cobb salad. "I miss the days where all we had to worry about was Jessa and what dark deeds she was up to."

"You do? Ugh, I don't." Laurie's eyes grew wide. "So,

the car—that vintage Corvette Harold had? That's what was stolen?"

Josephine nodded.

"I love that car. Poor Blanche must be at her wit's end with all this."

"At least Anton will be preoccupied hunting down that car instead of harassing Blanche for the time being," my daughter said.

I sipped my tea. "You know, I'm having a hard time deciding whether Harold's death was an accident or murder."

"What do you mean?" Laurie asked.

"I go back and forth constantly. I mean, look at all this loud fighting, public tantrums, punching cops—these are actions guaranteed to attract police scrutiny. If Ross or Anton were responsible, wouldn't they be acting more, I don't know... subtly? Keeping low profiles instead of causing regular chaotic scenes practically designed to be investigated as possible crimes?"

"You have a point. But you're also assuming that the culprits have a brain in their head. When crimes begin piling atop one another, it rarely indicates a brainiac from Smartron as a mastermind," Josephine said. She tapped a nail against her glass, expression sharp. "A dumb thief or murderer makes mistakes."

My gaze landed on Laurie, eyebrows knitting together. "You're awfully quiet. Everything okay?"

Laurie started slightly as if jolted from deep thought. "Oh! Yes, fine. I don't know, I haven't been all that involved in this one, so I'm playing catch up. Did Mario uncover anything actually helpful yet?"

"Nothing concrete yet," I answered.

"But soon. I can feel it," Josephine declared. "In my experience, desperate criminals lead investigators directly to the truth if one observes closely enough." A sly smile curved her lips. "And we excel at observing closely, do we not?"

A chorus of chuckles greeted this assessment as we clinked glasses.

After clearing away the lunch dishes, Laurie, Evie, Josephine, and I headed eagerly upstairs to the isolation room, hopeful we might gain new insights from questioning Nugget. As I eased open the door so as not to startle her, I said, "Nugget? I have some visitors with me. Is it okay if we come in and talk?"

Two ears perked up like radar dishes from behind a cozy cat tree, their soft fur twitching in anticipation. They were immediately followed by a pair of bright golden eyes peering out. Seeing me, Nugget scampered over, tail curled up happily.

Upon our entrance, Belladonna's body tensed like a coiled spring, and I could almost feel her fur bristle and rise as if a gentle electric current ran through her. From her elevated vantage point atop the cat tree, her eyes fixed on us with an intense stare, sharp as a hawk hunting its prey.

"Good afternoon, ladies," I said brightly. "We were hoping Nugget might be able to provide some insight to help us get to the bottom of everything happening with the Goldfinches."

Belladonna's eyes narrowed, but she remained silent and didn't attack anyone.

I took that as acceptance.

"Nugget, would you mind stepping onto the magic platter for a bit?" Evie asked gently. "That way, we can understand your answers."

Nugget hopped onto the plate, ears twitching curiously as she gazed at our small gathering.

"There's been so much confusion since your owner, Harold, died. We're trying to figure out exactly what happened, and we think you may have overheard or seen things that could help."

The calico's nose wrinkled. "Probably not. I don't listen much."

Evie exchanged a look with me.

"Don't be mad!" Nugget's ears drooped. "I'll try."

"We know you will, sweetie," I soothed. "Now, you mentioned a man came to argue with Harold a few days before he... went away forever. Was that man his brother, Anton?"

Again, at the sound of the name, Nugget crouched low, her fur puffing up in alarm. A distressed mewl escaped from her throat as her body tensed defensively.

"Sweetie, why are you so afraid of him?"

Tail tucked between her legs, Nugget let out another anxious cry, the haunted look in her eyes suggesting the name triggered traumatic memories. Though the plate glowed, she didn't say anything we could understand, and her whole body seemed to curl inward as she cowered.

"Okay, enough. You don't have to tell us if you don't want to," Josephine said. "Just nod yes or no if Harold's brother visited."

Nugget gave a hesitant nod, still hunkered down fearfully.

"Were they arguing?"

Another nod.

"About money?" Laurie asked.

Another tentative nod from Nugget.

"Did you see Harold's lawyer Ross Massey there that day, too?" I pressed gently. Nugget paused, then dipped her head again.

I exchanged a startled look with the others. This confirmed Anton and Ross were both at the shop right before Harold's death.

"That's very helpful information, sweetie," Josephine praised Nugget. Nugget's whiskers twitched with contentment as if sensing the rarity of such kind words from the usually sharp lawyer. "Now, I know this is difficult, but do you remember anything else unusual in the days before Harold died? Anything at all that seemed strange or worrisome?"

Nugget inquisitively tipped her head to the side, her earlier distress apparently forgotten. She peered up with curious eyes, now calm and pondering. "The food bowl got empty faster. And sometimes the water bowl was empty too, which never happens!" Her whiskers twitched in agitation.

I hid a smile.

That wasn't quite the bombshell reveal we'd hoped for.

"We appreciate you doing your best to remember," Laurie said kindly. "I know it's not easy."

Nugget seemed fully recovered, her short-term memory allowing her to move past the momentary fright. She said, "If you want to know human things, you should ask Mabel. She knows about Master Harold and everything to do with the coins and people coming to see him. She listens all the time. She's always around."

"Excellent idea," Josephine praised, stroking Nugget's back. The calico purred, mollified. "You've been a big help. Thank you for talking with us."

I shot Belladonna a conciliatory look as we prepared to leave. Her eyes narrowed to slits, and her ears flattened against her head aggressively until I said, "We appreciate your patience."

Bella's ears popped up.

The black cat studied me intently with her piercing yellow eyes, her gaze unblinking. After a long, tense moment, she finally broke her stare and inclined her head slowly, barely dipping her chin.

It wasn't much, but I'd take what I could get.

In the days since our tense conversation with Mabel, we had steered clear of approaching her again. To be blunt, after catching her deception about Anton's visit, she seemed as plausible a suspect as anyone in Harold's murder.

If it was a murder.

Which we still didn't know.

Just because Mabel appeared harmless on the outside didn't mean she was innocent, and we couldn't afford to ignore her any longer.

Chapter Thirteen

The late afternoon sun beat down on the dusty parking lot of Goldfinch Coins as Josephine, and I stepped out of my car. The "Closed" sign hung in the dark display window, but the front door stood slightly ajar. Faint light spilled out onto the sidewalk.

"I wonder why Blanche hasn't had Mabel reopen the shop yet," I said, pointing to a beat-up Ford in the parking lot. "That old Taurus is Mabel's."

"You sure?"

"I'm sure. She drove up in it the day Harold was killed and practically ran over the police when she forgot to put the thing in park. She must still be here even though the shop's closed."

Josephine shrugged elegantly. "All the more convenient for us. Shall we?"

Without waiting for an answer, she strode purposefully toward the door, her heels clicking rhythmically on the floor like a metronome of determination. As she reached the door, her hand elegantly grasped the handle, ready to open it with the same resolve she displayed in every aspect of her life.

"Wait." I hurried after her, glancing around the empty lot. "Maybe we should knock first? When Landon and I were here before, it looked like someone was sleeping in the office."

"It's unlocked. If we knock, we'll give her a chance to shoo us off," Josephine tutted, pushing the door open wider. "I think we go in."

The dim interior smelled musty and stale, like a place that hadn't been aired out properly in days. As my eyes adjusted to the gloom, I saw clutter and dust coating the display cases that usually sparkled under Mabel's fastidious care.

Mabel sat slumped at a desk in the cramped back office, staring vacantly at a computer screen. She looked utterly disheveled, her lank hair escaping its bun and her oversized cardigan wrinkled. Dark circles shadowed her eyes. At our entrance, she leaped up in surprise.

"Oh! I'm so sorry, but the shop's closed," she stammered, smoothing her skirt with trembling hands. "I should have locked up, but I must have forgotten."

"That's quite all right, dear," Josephine said briskly, ignoring Mabel's obvious discomfort. "We're not here to shop. Just to have a chat."

Mabel paled, gaze darting between us. "Oh, well, I-I don't know if that's..."

"We won't take up much of your time," I said gently. Mabel's anxious demeanor made me want to put her at ease. "We just had a few quick questions."

"About... about Nugget?" Mabel asked faintly, blinking back tears. "Is she doing okay?"

Josephine's sharp gaze took in the disarray. "Among other things, yes. The cat's fine. Probably better where she is since you clearly have quite a lot going on here yourself." She gestured at the cluttered office. "Cataloging the inventory Harold left behind?"

"I... well, I've just been trying to keep myself busy," Mabel stammered. "To keep my mind occupied."

"Understandable. His death must have come as a terrible shock." Josephine's tone turned syrupy and sweet. "Especially after so many years as his loyal assistant."

Mabel's eyes filled with tears behind her glasses. "It's been dreadful. I can hardly believe he's gone." She reached for a tissue, dabbing at her eyes.

Part of me wanted to comfort this gentle, unassuming woman so obviously grieving a dear friend. But logic cautioned me not to accept her meek persona at face value. However harmless she appeared, too many questions surrounded Mabel to dismiss her as innocent.

I cleared my throat gently. "We know this is difficult, but we were hoping you could clarify a few things about events leading up to Harold's death."

"Events?" Mabel froze, tissue clutched in her trembling hand. "But I don't know anything." Despite her denial, panic shone in her eyes.

"Now, now, no need to be shy." Josephine wandered deeper into the office, gazing idly around. "We're simply trying to make sense of some peculiar inconsistencies regarding the days before the accident."

"For the cat?" Mabel asked faintly.

Josephine ignored her question. "For instance, I understand you mentioned previously that Anton Goldfinch came by that Thursday. Yet you later claimed it was just a phone call." Josephine glanced over her shoulder. "Which was it?"

"I-I'm not sure what you mean." Mabel twisted the tissue, shredding it between anxious fingers. "It's all so muddled lately."

"Muddled how?"

Mabel just shook her head wordlessly, lower lip trembling.

Josephine sighed. "Let's speak plainly, shall we? Harold is dead under suspicious circumstances. The police investigation appears deliberately impeded. Valuables go missing, tantrums ensue, and you show up at the cat rescue for a political fundraiser trying to seem normal when you are clearly anything but."

Mabel flinched at the lawyer's matter-of-fact recap.

"Something sinister lurks beneath the surface here," Josephine pressed on, "and we simply want to uncover the truth. Help us do right by Harold's memory."

Not the way I would've approached it, but Josephine

did have all the subtly of a sledgehammer. And to my utter shock?

It seemed to work.

Tears now spilled down Mabel's cheeks. "Harold was a good man. Truly, he was. But he trusted the wrong people." She drew a shaky breath. "He meant well with that coin venture, but it brought out ugliness in those around him."

I exchanged a startled glance with Josephine. This was more than Mabel had revealed yet.

"What ugliness?" I asked gently. "We know Anton argued with Harold that day. And that Ross Massey came here. What was happening?"

"And what coin venture?" Josephine asked.

Mabel just shook her head, looking cornered. "I shouldn't say more. Please, I want no part in this nastiness." She moved toward the office door. "Now I really must insist you both leave."

"We're not here to upset you. But we need to understand if you know anything that could explain the strange events since Harold's death." I softened my voice further and thanked my lucky stars she didn't ask me why we needed to understand anything. "Help us understand who deleted the security footage in the shopping center that day. You know more about this store than anyone."

At that, Mabel froze. "Security footage?" She paled further. "Deleted?"

"You didn't know?" I asked gently. As I spoke to

Mabel, Josephine perused the shelf of knick-knacks on the side of the office. She picked up one item, examined it, then placed it back down only to pick up one more. "The recording of that day disappeared somehow. Anything you could share about who was here might prove critical."

Mabel seemed to fold in on herself, shoulders hunching. "I don't know who could have... I mean, I... oh, that's dreadful." She sank into the desk chair, shaking her head. "This is precisely why I wanted no part of their plan. Mr. Goldfinch refused to listen when I warned him it would lead to no good end."

"Warned him about what?" Josephine pressed, turning away from the display shelves. "Mabel, just tell us plainly what sort of trouble Harold was in."

Mabel just gazed at the floor, despair etched on her face. "Please, please go. I've said too much already."

Josephine cast one last speculative look around the dim office before allowing me to usher her into the parking lot. We exited the cool shadowy interior into the blazing noonday sun. I squinted against the sudden brightness as Josephine slipped on a pair of large sunglasses.

"Well, that was enlightening," she remarked as we headed for my car. "The plot thickens by the minute in this sordid affair."

"Enlightening? I don't feel enlightened."

"You're not very good at this, are you?" Josephine said. "She's clearly scared and hiding something big, but she also doesn't know about key aspects of the cover-up. She didn't know the footage had been deleted, and the fact that it had? It clearly alarmed her. Call me crazy, but I don't think Mabel's a calculating criminal mastermind capable of murder."

"No," I agreed. "If she is guilty of anything, I'd wager it's being too blindly loyal and trusting of the wrong people."

We reached the car, and I glanced back at the coin shop, its darkened windows like so many unanswered questions. With a sigh, I slid behind the wheel. "Either way, it seems poor Harold Goldfinch got in over his head in something dangerous. And it may have cost him his life."

"Indeed." Josephine fastened her seatbelt, lips pursed in thought. "We just need to find out what it is even though everyone involved is afraid to talk to us or claims they don't know anything."

Moments after I started the car, the soft crunch of tires rolling over gravel caught our attention. Both of us glanced up as another vehicle pulled into the lot, parking a few spots away.

It was a sleek black luxury SUV, shiny and imposing. As it came to a stop, the driver's door swung open. Anton Goldfinch unfolded his tall frame from the front seat, emerging from the high vehicle with all the elegant grace his personality lacked.

His gaze landed on our idling car, eyes narrowing.

"What are you doing here?" he shouted at me without preamble. He was loud enough that I could hear him through the closed windows. "Everywhere I turn, you're in my face."

I tensed, exchanging an uneasy glance with Josephine. "That's Anton Goldfinch, Harold's crazy brother."

Without responding, Josephine opened her door and stepped out gracefully. "Why, Mr. Goldfinch, what a coincidence running into you here. We simply stopped by to offer our condolences to poor Mabel. I'm sure this must be a terribly difficult time for her as well as you."

I turned off the engine, got out of the car, and moved to stand next to her.

Anton's eyes narrowed, unconvinced. "At this hour?"

This hour?

It was the middle of the afternoon.

On a Tuesday.

"Seems to me you people in Tablerock have an odd habit of sticking your noses where they don't belong." His glare bounced between us. "You seem to keep turning up around my family's private affairs. Makes me wonder what you're really up to."

I bristled at his confrontational tone but fought to keep

my voice even. "This is a small town, Mr. Goldfinch. In a big city like Las Vegas, you may not be nearly as tight-knit as we are, but we are a community in Tablerock. We care about folks and know when outsiders come and go in our town."

If what I said rattled him, he didn't show it.

Anton took a few steps closer, using his impressive height to loom over me. "Yeah? Doesn't seem that way to me. I heard about how you ladies treated Mabel last night." He jerked his chin toward the shop. "Now, why don't you tell me what you're really doing here?"

I resisted the urge to throttle this obnoxious bully.

Drawing a calming breath, I met his gaze steadily. "As Josephine said, we merely came to pay our respects to Mabel. Nothing more."

Anton looked anything but convinced. His lip curled derisively. "Right. Because you two are such great friends with my brother's mousy assistant."

"Perhaps we are," Josephine said archly. "Or perhaps her well-being concerns us after the tragic loss of her employer."

Anton crossed his arms. "Yeah, well, her well-being is none of your concern. This is family business." He took another step closer, using his bulk to intimidate us.

I refused to be cowed. "Mr. Goldfinch, I understand you're grieving, but there's no call for this hostility," I said evenly. "We'll be on our way and leave you in peace."

Anton glowered but seemed to realize making a scene in public wouldn't serve his purposes. With visible effort, he reined in his temper. "Yeah, see that you do." His lip curled in a sneer. "Wouldn't want any more trouble around here." He paused. "If you get my meaning."

With that vaguely threatening parting shot, he turned on his heel and stalked toward the coin shop entrance. I watched his hulking frame disappear inside, pulse-pounding with anger and unease.

Josephine arched one elegant eyebrow. "Well, he's certainly charming." She shook her head. "That man doesn't have a diplomatic bone in his body." Josephine pointed. "Go park over there, behind that tree. We need to be close."

"For what?"

Josephine's tablet displayed a crisp HD video feed inside the shadowy coin shop. Mabel still sat slumped at her desk, head cradled in her hands.

"You bugged the coin shop?" I gasped, stunned by this development.

"Bugged is such a loaded word," Josephine dismissed my concern with a wave of her hand.

I frowned. "Isn't that illegal?"

"Generally, if a private property is open to the public, like a store, you can record unless expressly prohibited." Josephine kept her gaze locked on the video. "I didn't see a sign posted, did you?"

I shifted uneasily. "Well, no, but..."

"There you have it then." Josephine tapped the screen. "We're observing a public spot with a perfectly legal camera, and we're within range of the Wi-Fi, so we're not remotely observing. This is legal." She shrugged. "Well, it's arguable, at least. Ethically debatable, but legal and effective. Now hush and watch."

At the sound of Anton's approach, Mabel started up in dismay.

"Oh! Mr. Goldfinch." She pressed a hand to her chest, eyes wide and frightened. "I didn't realize you were— That is... What brings you by?"

Anton glowered, clearly still seething from his confrontation with us. "Never mind why I'm here. I want to know why those two busybodies keep sniffing around." He braced his hands on Mabel's desk, looming over her. "What exactly did they want?"

Mabel shrank back, wringing her hands anxiously. "N-nothing, sir, truly." At Anton's deepening scowl, she added, "They simply offered condolences for Harold's passing."

We didn't want him to know what we asked about, but neither did Mabel.

Anton's hand slammed down on the desk, making Mabel jump. "Don't lie to me! I'm not stupid." He leaned closer, menacing. "They're up to something. Poking their noses where they don't belong."

Mabel trembled, clasping her hands as if in prayer.

"Please, I think they're just concerned. I didn't tell them anything. I swear."

"Oh yeah?" Anton's hands closed into fists. "Then why do you look ready to wet yourself, huh?" He took a step back, beginning to pace as his temper rose. "You know what I think? I think you've been talking. Telling tales to the whole damn town!" His voice rose to a shout. "Trying to make me look guilty for what happened to my brother."

Mabel cringed at his volume, shaking her head frantically. "No, I wouldn't do that. I promise."

He smacked his fist into his palm, causing Mabel to flinch again. "Someone's talking. And you're the only one who knew I was in town when my brother took a header off that ladder." Anton's expression contorted in fury, his next shout blistering. "Are you trying to set me up?"

All color drained from Mabel's face. "N-no, please," she stammered. "I'd never—"

"Shut it!" Anton bellowed. "I don't want to hear any more of your pathetic sniveling."

He stormed to the front of the shop, flinging open the door. "Keep your mouth shut if you know what's good for you. If you breathe a word about our family business to anyone, you'll regret it. Understand?"

Mabel gave a faint, jerky nod, her face a mask of fear.

Anton suddenly slammed the door with explosive force.

The entire video frame shook with the impact.

In the office, Mabel flinched violently at the deafening bang. For an instant, stark terror contorted her features. Just as quickly, she stifled the reaction, resuming her weary slump. But her hands now clutched each other, bloodless and shaking.

His SUV roared as he sped out of the parking lot.

Beside me, Josephine clicked her tongue. "Well, that was illuminating."

I put the car in drive, rolling slowly from the lot. "I'll say. He did it."

"Well, he's part of it. So is she." Josephine frowned. "The question is, what do we do now? Confronting that horrid Anton again seems unwise until we know more."

Josephine tapped a nail against the window as she pondered. "What if we paid a visit to that odious Ross Massey? He clearly knows more than he's letting on."

I frowned uncertainly. "What excuse would we have to go visit him?"

"Nugget, obviously." Josephine looked affronted. "We'll have to be more subtle than that."

"Subtle, how?" I asked warily. Something told me her definition and my definition differed greatly.

"We'll simply inquire about reviewing Harold's will on behalf of the cat." At my skeptical look, she added airily, "As Nugget's current guardians, it's perfectly reasonable we'd want to verify any stipulations regarding her care and who can visit her. I am the shelter's lawyer. This all sounds perfectly reasonable."

I had to admit it seemed like a decent premise to justify the visit.

"Won't he see right through that excuse?"

"Of course, he will," Josephine said, as though this were obvious. "We're relying on that arrogant man's ego. He'll assume we're there to beg crumbs of information about the estate from him, and he'll enjoy making me flatter him."

"But he knows we suspect foul play. Won't he be instantly on guard?"

"Let me handle that," Josephine said breezily. "I know how to stroke these egos to get them talking."

"Okay." I still wasn't fully convinced, but we were running out of options. "I guess it's worth a try. But if he sees through it—"

"Please," Josephine scoffed. "That two-bit shyster got his law degree from an online college. He couldn't out-maneuver a stray dog."

Chapter Fourteen

As we pulled into the lot behind Ross Massey's modest law office, the plainness of the building was immediately apparent. It was a dull, rectangular box constructed of faded brown bricks that blended into the drab backdrop. The entire structure exuded austerity, devoid of any embellishments or architectural flair.

The walkway to the entrance—cracked and weed-strewn, with no flower or shrub—led to a small sign by the dingy door announcing "Ross Massey, Attorney at Law" in no-nonsense black lettering. Even the sign was weathered and peeling at the edges.

No one in Harold Goldfinch's life seemed to match his success.

As we headed inside, I shot Josephine a sidelong look. "Please just... try not to provoke him too much, all right? We need information from him, and riling him up will get us nowhere."

She blinked, the picture of innocence. "Oh, Ellie, you know me. I'm the soul of tact."

Before I could tell her I knew that was not the case, she swept inside, moving with smooth confidence. I followed, already steeling myself for the battle of veiled words and wits I expected was inevitable.

I mean, the two were both lawyers, after all.

At our entrance, the receptionist's eyes ballooned, clearly recognizing the infamous Josephine Reynolds, attorney at law. Before she could react, Josephine swept past her desk with a patronizing smile.

"No need to announce us," she purred. "We just need a quick chat with Mr. Massey."

Flustered, the poor receptionist hurried after us down the hall. "I'm sorry, but do you have an appointment? Mr. Massey is quite busy—"

Josephine waved a dismissive hand, cutting off the spluttering woman's objections. "We won't keep him long, I assure you."

I shot the receptionist an apologetic look as Josephine rapped sharply on the office door. That woman was only trying to do her job, and Josephine had barged right past as if she were insignificant.

Without waiting for a response, Josephine swept inside.

I trailed uncertainly after her, nerves jangling.

We were essentially ambushing Ross Massey, Harold's lawyer, on what I thought was a bit of a flimsy premise.

I hoped Josephine knew what she was doing.

Ross Massey sat behind an ornate wood desk, speaking irritably on the phone. He looked up in surprise as we entered, then his expression clouded over.

"I'll have to call you back," he bit out, hanging up abruptly.

Josephine flashed a dazzling, close-lipped smile. "Mr. Massey, so good of you to see us on short notice." Without waiting for an invitation, she gracefully settled into one of the tufted leather chairs across from him.

I hovered awkwardly near the door, now offering Ross an apologetic shrug, my shoulders rising sheepishly as I tried to convey through gesture that this ambush wasn't my idea.

Ross's icy stare bounced between us, making it clear our impromptu arrival was about as welcome as a porcupine at a balloon convention. I shot him another sheepish, pleading look, hoping he'd direct his annoyance at the steamrolling lawyer orchestrating this ambush, not the hapless accomplice hovering awkwardly against the wall.

"To what do I owe the pleasure, Josephine?" he asked flatly, sarcasm dripping from each syllable.

Josephine leaned forward, interlacing her manicured fingers. "Well, you see, an urgent matter has arisen regarding Harold's estate that requires clarification," she began smoothly. "As Nugget's temporary guardians, we must ensure we abide by Harold's wishes for her care."

I held my breath, watching Ross closely. His eyes

instantly narrowed with suspicion at Josephine's thinly veiled pretense.

"No one has told us specifics about any provisions Harold made for Nugget in his will," Josephine continued breezily. "Naturally, reviewing the documents would provide the easiest solution."

She left the implication that Ross could shed light on the will's contents as Harold's lawyer if one existed. I struggled to keep a neutral expression, hoping against hope he'd take the bait. We were relying on that arrogant man's ego to assume we'd come begging him for crumbs of information.

Ross sat back, steepling his fingers as he eyed Josephine shrewdly. "I see. You just wish to verify the provisions Harold outlined regarding his cat." Smug satisfaction crept into his smile. "A reasonable concern, I suppose."

He had taken the bait, exactly as Josephine predicted. In fact, he seemed positively tickled by the notion we'd come begging him for information.

Which was... weird.

"Then you can provide a copy of the will?" Josephine pressed. "Excellent."

Ross made an exaggerated expression of regret. "Ah, well, that's the trouble, you see. I've yet to locate the final executed documents."

Josephine blinked, feigning confusion. "No executed will? How peculiar." She tilted her head. "When did you last review a draft with Harold?"

"It's been some time," Ross said evasively.

"But you must have discussed his intentions at some point as his lawyer, right?" I asked. "Do you know who he wanted to take possession of Nugget? Was there any provision at all made for her care?"

Ross's smug smile faded, annoyance flashing across his features at my probing questions. "On occasion, yes—though I prefer to keep client conversations confidential. Since it's the law."

"Of course," Josephine jumped in, smoothing his ruffled feathers. "We understand completely. But I need to point out that you were Harold's trusted counsel for many years, and we are just talking about a cat here. We don't need to see the papers themselves. It would ease our minds if you could provide insight into Nugget's provisions. You are the only one that can, after all..."

She left the thought dangling irresistibly, and Ross's expression turned smug once more at the implications of his importance in the silence that followed.

"Well, I suppose I could provide some... general insight on that topic without violating privilege," he acquiesced.

Violating privilege?

Harold was dead. What privilege could the guy possibly have?

Ross leaned back in his leather chair, steepling his fingers once more. "Between you and me, Harold never cared much for that cat one way or another. Nugget was more his assistant Mabel's pet than his. So he didn't make any provisions for the cat. I mean, it's a cat."

Josephine and I exchanged a surprised glance at this revelation.

"Are you sure?" I asked.

Ross nodded his head. "I assure you, Harold's will is focused on distributing his considerable assets to those he cared about and says nothing about a cat." As if reminded of something unpleasant, Ross grimaced and rubbed his forearm.

I noticed for the first time an angry red gash marring his skin.

"That animal is nothing but trouble if you ask me," he continued. "Just look what she did to my arm when I visited Harold last week!" He shook his head in disgust. "You ladies can do whatever you please with her. Put her down for all I care. Harold certainly never made any arrangements for her."

I swallowed my scathing retort, keeping my expression neutral. Antagonizing Ross wouldn't get us anywhere, I reminded myself. We had to loosely string this puffed up blowhard along, at least for now.

Josephine, meanwhile, nodded along sympathetically. "How dreadful that the animal lashed out at you that way! We appreciate you taking the time to clarify the matter for us."

She stood gracefully, extending her hand to Ross with a polite smile that didn't reach her eyes. "Well, we won't take up any more of your valuable time today. You've been most helpful."

I didn't think he'd been helpful at all.

Ross looked momentarily taken aback as Josephine abruptly announced we'd be departing. Clearly, he'd expected more fawning and flattery in return for the meager crumbs of insight he'd provided.

Ross recovered quickly, standing to return her brisk handshake with a tight smile. But I caught the flash of annoyance in his eyes at having his self-important blathering cut short.

"Well, thank you for your time, Mr. Massey," Josephine said smoothly.

I echoed her thanks, resisting the urge to punch him in the nose as I followed Josephine out. Put down Nugget?

The nerve of that man.

"But we didn't learn anything," I told her.

"Of course we did."

The late afternoon sun slanted through the windshield as we drove back to the Silver Circle Cat Shelter. "Okay, we learned that oily eel is clearly full of more hot air than a leaky balloon. I'll give you that."

"We learned more than that. We learned he's lying."

I glanced at her questioningly. "You don't believe

what he said about there being no provisions for Nugget in the will?"

"Not for one moment. I visited Harold at his shop. He loved that cat." Josephine shook her head, lips pursed in disdain. "Massey is a two-bit shyster at best. Lying comes as naturally as breathing to him."

"But why would he lie about that?" I wondered aloud.

"Who can fathom the motives of these unscrupulous sorts?" Josephine waved a hand dismissively. "Though I'd wager it has something to do with money. It always does. You're forgetting something, though. Something you told me is at odds with what Massey told us."

I glanced at her.

Josephine prompted me with an arched eyebrow. "Think, Ellie. Surely you didn't forget what Blanche told you and Landon about Harold's will."

The memory of my conversation with Blanche suddenly came flooding back, and Josephine was right. What she'd told me was completely at odds with Ross's claim that Harold had a will at all.

"Blanche told us they had no will," I said. "That there wasn't one yet because they never got around to it. She even said she and Harold had an appointment scheduled for the following week to begin the process."

"Exactly." She tapped a nail against the window ledge. "Someone isn't being truthful. Either Blanche lied about the lack of a will, or that reptilian Ross lied about its existence."

I frowned. "But why? What would either gain by lying?"

"An excellent question." Josephine pursed her lips. "Though at the moment, pure speculation. We need more facts and information before figuring out who's up to no good here."

As the cat shelter's welcoming sign appeared, we lapsed into contemplative silence again, but as I turned into the long drive, Josephine spoke again. "Mark my words. We will get to the bottom of this."

I smiled at her determination as we stopped, eager to confer with the others about this newest twist.

The late afternoon sun streamed through the large windows of the cat shelter's third floor penthouse. Soft meows and purrs filled the air as cats wound lazily around our feet, vying for attention.

Landon, Laurie, Evie, Josephine, and I sat in a loose circle on the plush cushions scattered around the penthouse lounge area, keeping our voices low as we debated the maze of contradictory details unearthed so far.

"Where's Matt this evening?" I asked Evie, noticing his absence.

"Oh, he's at some private investigator training seminar," my daughter replied.

Josephine nodded approvingly. "Excellent. Perhaps he'll learn investigative techniques we can put to use."

From Josephine's mouth to God's ears. I hoped Matt would come back armed with insider tricks of the trade and point out better ways for us to go about this. We could use all the help we could get untangling the web surrounding Harold Goldfinch's demise, and right now, I felt like a pinball getting randomly pinged around.

Laurie sighed, absently stroking the tabby curled in her lap. "Well, for now, it's just us, and I don't know how we're supposed to figure this out. Everyone seems to have a different version of events." The cat purred softly, eyes closed in bliss, as Laurie's fingers automatically scratched behind its ears.

I shook my head in frustration as I stroked a silky Persian. My nails scratched lightly at it, eliciting louder rumbles of pleasure even as my frustration mounted. "There must be some thread of truth connecting it all. We just have to find it, right?"

"Easier said than done when no one's telling the truth," Landon pointed out. He gently lifted the insistent tuxedo cat off his lap, placing it on the ground despite its protests. As soon as its paws hit the floor, the cat sprang back up, scrambling with dexterous agility onto his shoulder.

"Really?" Landon asked it.

From its perch, the cat meowed loudly right by his ear as if scolding him for the eviction. With a resigned sigh, Landon reached up to scratch it behind the ears in acquiescence, allowing the willful creature to maintain its post upon his shoulder.

Josephine snapped her fingers. "Look. I believe it's time we change tactics," she declared. "All this poking about and interrogating people clearly isn't getting us anywhere."

I looked at Josephine curiously. "So, what do you suggest?"

Her lips curved into a sly, crafty smile. "We handle this the proper Southern lady way—with sugar, not vinegar."

Landon's forehead creased in confusion. "Come again?"

"No more strong-arming our suspects," Josephine said smoothly, her voice dripping sweet as honey. She tapped her chin. "We'll bake a pie or two, pay a friendly little visit to the coin shop, and help poor Mabel tidy up."

Josephine emphasized "friendly" and "help" with faux sincerity, laying on the sugary charm. Leaning close, her eyes glinted deviously as she pretended to inspect her manicure.

"While we're there, we'll just oh-so-subtly chat and peek at every scrap of paper we can get our hands on."

I frowned, shaking my head. "You want to trick her into gossiping while we snoop around under the guise of helping her?"

"You make it sound so devious," Josephine responded, waving her hand dismissively. "It's merely leveraging the tools at our disposal. The cat doesn't know much, so we have to work with what we have." She flashed an exaggerated smile and batted her eyelashes. "A little pie and light conversation—what could be more harmless?"

Evie chuckled, drawling exaggeratedly, "Kill 'em with kindness. It's the Texas way."

Josephine nodded approvingly, pointing at Evie. "Exactly. We have to stop pretending we're some kind of Sherlock Holmes dream team. We're bouncing back and forth and finding nothing concrete."

She had a point. Our amateur sleuthing attempts kept leading nowhere. But tricking a grieving, fragile woman like Mabel into betraying confidences didn't sit right with me either.

"Let's just keep thinking," I suggested diplomatically. "Maybe there's a way we can get information without manipulating Mabel."

"I don't know, Mom," Evie said. "I think it's a good idea."

"If she's not guilty of anything or part of some conspiracy, we are really helping her," Laurie pointed out. "No one else is because of all the rumors flying around town. The poor woman is completely isolated and alone."

"And, Ellie, all we're doing is running in circles finding nothing concrete," Josephine said, pacing. "We need to change the game."

Chapter Fifteen

THE COMFORTING AROMA OF CINNAMON AND nutmeg filled the air as I rolled out another sheet of pie dough across the flour-dusted counter. Around me, the cozy kitchen buzzed with lighthearted chatter and laughter, a welcome reprieve after the intense events of the past week.

Josephine stood at the stove, wooden spoon in hand, intently stirring a bubbling pot of apple filling destined for one of the three pies we were assembling. She paused to take a sip of Merlot, then gestured theatrically with her wine glass.

"You know, Ellie, I have to ask—isn't your carpenter pining for your company while we ladies have pie night?" She arched one perfectly sculpted eyebrow. "I don't think I've seen the two of you apart for more than six hours since you started dating."

I chuckled, drizzling olive oil over a second round of

dough. "Oh, I'm sure Landon can find ways to occupy his time when I'm busy. He's not exactly the clingy, needy type."

"That's true. Neither is my Charlie," Josephine replied airily with a tinkling laugh. "I can't even recall the last time I spent a full evening at home with the man. It's good to have a husband that revels in his alone time."

Laurie, who was slicing apples with brisk efficiency, shot Josephine a skeptical look. "Really? Doesn't it ever bother your husband for you two to spend so much time apart?"

"Of course not." Josephine waved her hand as if swatting the notion away like a gnat. "We're both perfectly content in our little arrangement. I have my life and commitments, he has his, and we come together when it suits us." She took another dainty sip of wine. "It's quite liberating, actually. No tedious expectations."

I exchanged an amused glance with Laurie across the granite-topped kitchen island as we listened to Josephine chat breezily about her unique approach to marriage.

Josephine's tendency to view her husband Charlie more as an occasional fixture than a life partner was puzzling to me. But despite their independent lives, their unconventional dynamic seemed to work for the pair.

I offered Laurie a knowing smile and shrug, deciding Josephine's unique marital philosophy wasn't worth debating. Our friend marched to the beat of her own drummer in all aspects of life—why should matrimony be any different?

Laurie just shook her head, dredging the apple slices through a bowl of cinnamon sugar. "I can't imagine Harold and Blanche had that kind of modern arrangement. From what she's said in the past, it sounds like they mostly led separate lives by default rather than conscious choice. She was never happy about it."

I carefully transferred the dough rounds into waiting pie pans. "No, she wasn't. She mentioned something about it to us—Landon and me—at Waldo's barbecue before Harold passed. She always seemed unhappy that he would obsess over his business."

My words hung in the air as we lapsed into contemplative silence, hands busy with our culinary tasks.

Finally, Josephine tutted, depositing her emptied wine glass on the counter with a definitive clink.

"Well, I don't think Blanche killed him, so there is no need to obsess over her. For one, she was at that barbecue all day. Two, whatever their faults as a couple, Blanche loved Harold. Anyone could see that."

Muffled laughter drifted from behind Evie's closed door.

"You let Matt go into her room with the door closed?" Laurie asked.

"I trust my daughter. Besides, she's not a teenager. Evie's almost twenty-five. How am I supposed to tell her she can't have a young man in her room?"

"You say it just like that," Laurie joked.

"Matt and Evie wouldn't disrespect Ellie like that, and you know it. Besides, if they were going to stoke a particular fire, that young man would spring for the Regal Mirage in downtown Austin at the very least. I'm sure of it." Josephine's smile turned wistful. "Your daughter and Matt really do seem perfect for each other."

I chuckled at her euphemism as I crimped the pie crust edges. "They do spend nearly every free moment together. I swear those two even text nonstop during school and work."

"That's young love for you." Josephine sighed dramatically. "All consuming. I remember those days well."

"Somehow, I have a hard time picturing you consumed by anything, Josephine," Laurie teased.

Josephine gasped in exaggerated offense. "Is it so impossible to believe I was once a starry-eyed, boy-crazy young woman like any other?"

Laurie and I both chuckled at the mental image of a lovesick teenage Josephine mooning over some gangly, pimply prom date.

"Oh, I'm sure you had your share of crushes," I assured her. "It's just that you always seem so..."

"Restrained?" Laurie suggested diplomatically.

I nodded agreement, still chuckling. "Composed. Unflappable."

"Yes, exactly," Laurie chimed in. "I can't see any crush knocking your perfectly poised feathers out of place."

Josephine huffed, but her eyes sparkled with amusement. "Well, I'll have you know I harbored quite the passion for debate team captain Calvin Huxley in high school." She leaned in conspiratorially. "The balcony scene from Romeo and Juliet was mere child's play next to the romantic dramatics I concocted trying to seduce that oblivious boy."

"Wait a minute. Calvin Huxley, the state representative?" I asked, surprised.

"The very one."

Our laughter rose again at the thought of serious, practical Josephine as a lovesick teen. I wondered if she had really been so different then or if she simply enjoyed spinning an exaggerated tale for our benefit now.

"Did you ever manage to catch the young man's eye?" Laurie asked.

"His affections were bound to Rebecca Allerton, head cheerleader and homecoming queen." Josephine heaved a theatrical sigh. "My broken heart found solace in study and achievement instead. Which was a good thing—it's not easy to get into UT."

"Probably for the best," I said wryly, rotating the finished pie crusts. "I think his current wife's name is Tiffany. Tammy? Anyway, can you imagine Josephine Reynolds as a politician's devoted wife?"

Laurie chuckled. "Only in some alternative universe."

"I take offense to that." Josephine lifted her chin. "I'd

be a fantastic politician's wife. Did you ever watch House of Cards? You know the wife that supplanted her husband?"

Laurie and I nodded.

"I could run circles around her."

Her imperious words drew fresh chuckles from Laurie and me. Josephine allowed herself an amused smile at our mirth.

"In all seriousness, you're quite right," she acknowledged. "The more traditional supportive mate role would never have satisfied me." Josephine moved the bubbling pot off the burner, slipping on oven mitts. "If not for Charlie's gracious willingness to accommodate my ambitions, I likely would've divorced as often as Liz Taylor."

I swung open the oven door. "I think the pies are ready for the oven. Let's get them baking so we can talk strategy."

Josephine nodded briskly. "I'll fetch Evie and Matt from her room."

"You're just trying to catch them in a compromising position."

"Compromising? I'm trying to catch them naked."

"Josephine!" I swatted at her with a dish towel while she cackled.

I slid the pie-laden baking sheets into the oven and closed the door.

"Perfect timing," Josephine declared, glancing at the timer. "Just enough minutes to finalize our strategy for tomorrow before they're ready."

She turned to the kitchen table, where Evie was already seated with a notepad. Laurie and I joined them, ready to hammer out our game plan.

"Operation Dessert Offensive is a go," Evie said with mock seriousness, clicking her pen.

Josephine nodded approvingly. "I do so enjoy your whimsical approach to these escapades, my dear." Her expression turned shrewd. "Where did Matt go?"

"Early class tomorrow," Evie explained as I gathered dishes from the table to give us room.

Josephine gave a thoughtful hum. "I would have thought his new role as a private investigator would provide us more benefit by now."

"It will. He's still in training," Evie reminded her. "Give him time to figure out which end is up."

"Nonsense. Matt should just jump in with both feet."

Evie rolled her eyes.

"All right, just us ladies then," Josephine said decisively. "Now, what's our premise for this little visit?" she asked like it was a pop quiz.

"To help Mabel tidy up the shop and have a nice chat," I said.

"While also subtly fishing for any information to advance our investigation," Laurie added.

"Exactly. Idle gossip can grease many wheels," Josephine said airily. "And if certain details just happen to slip out as we tidy the place, so much the better."

She leaned forward, steepling her manicured fingers. "The key will be quickly gaining her trust and allaying suspicions about our motives for being there. Though I doubt she'll have any thanks to the pies." Josephine tapped her chin thoughtfully. "Perhaps we should also bring cleaning supplies to really sell the ruse?"

I considered this. "It's probably not a bad idea. What are we looking for, though? Are we just hoping Mabel will be so grateful we're there that she spills her guts? Or are we going to look through the papers to see if we can find a motive for murder?"

Laurie nodded in agreement. "I'd say yes to everything she just said, no?"

"The mousy assistant is keeping secrets. Whether it's because she's guilty, because she's covering for someone guilty, or because she's been threatened into silence, there's no way to know," Josephine said, eyes glinting. "Not until we get over there and start talking to her and poking around."

Ambushing the unsuspecting (and grieving) woman with pies and nosy questions still didn't sit totally right with my conscience. But we were at a dead end in unraveling who committed this crime, and Josephine was likely right. Mabel seemed to be in the middle of this somehow.

Josephine seemed to read my thoughts. "Ellie Rockwell, stop it. Desperate times occasionally call for creative measures. The ends will justify our pretty innocuous means." Her knowing gaze traveled over each of us in turn, expression solemn. "And if we find out this is all nothing, we've helped the girl and taken a burden from her. What could be wrong with that?"

I straightened my spine, nodding. "That's true. Okay, I can fret over ethics later. For now, let's figure out our exact plan of attack tomorrow."

Josephine's eyes glowed triumphantly, like a general steeling her soldiers for battle. "I don't know why you ever doubt me." She gestured for Evie to slide the notepad and pen over. "Now, let's make a checklist of the cleaning supplies we'll need."

The oven timer dinged, interrupting Josephine mid-list.

I rose quickly to extract the golden, bubbling pies before they were over-baked, and the mouthwatering smell of warm fruit and flaky crust filled the kitchen. If nothing else, at least our visit tomorrow would yield Mabel the comfort of a tasty treat and helping hands during a difficult time.

Once the pies cooled sufficiently on the stovetop, I began slicing the extra one we'd made for us while Josephine resumed issuing orders for our clandestine operation.

"...and Ellie, you'll take point conversing with Mabel. Laurie and I will wander a bit, tidying and keeping an eye out for anything of interest." She tapped her chin. "Remember, we're looking for any paperwork, files, notes—anything that could provide insight into Harold's business affairs and relationships."

I nodded, scooping vanilla ice cream onto our dessert plates. "Hopefully, she won't be too suspicious if we poke around while cleaning. People tend to get distracted and shuffle through papers when tidying up."

Josephine smiled approvingly, accepting her dish. "Precisely. A natural impulse we can leverage." She took an eager bite of the warm pie, closing her eyes in bliss. "Mmm. Superb. Ellie, you should sell these in the café."

Laurie and Evie echoed her praise as they dug in.

I looked at her. "I'm glad you all like them, but I couldn't. I would never have any time."

"It's really a shame," she said with her mouth full.

I allowed myself a small, proud smile at their enthusiasm.

I nearly dropped my fork as Laurie's suggestion registered, certain I must be hallucinating.

"You want to bring Nugget and the magic platter to the possible murder scene?" I repeated in disbelief. "Did someone slip something into your drink?"

"Think about it," Laurie said eagerly, eyes glowing

with excitement. "We'd get instant access to anything Nugget overheard that could be relevant. No guessing what she remembers. She could just tell us directly."

"And when Mabel pulls out the shop shotgun in a panic at the talking cat and magic plate, that will go just splendidly," I said.

Evie looked at me curiously. "How do you know the store has a gun, Mom?"

"This is Texas, Evie," I responded. "Grocery stores here have guns, and the coin shop has valuable merchandise. I'd be more surprised if there wasn't a loaded handgun behind that counter."

Evie's eyes widened. "Seriously? I kinda thought that was just a stereotype."

I shook my head solemnly. "Oh no, it's very much real. Most businesses around here are armed and ready for action." I gestured out the window. "Old Tom's Feed Store probably has enough firepower to take down an invading militia."

Evie laughed.

Laurie, Josephine, and I did not.

Evie's laughter petered out uncertainly. "Wait, you guys aren't serious... right?" she asked, eyes darting between us.

"Have you met Old Tom?" I asked, thinking of his rough and tumble appearance, ample beer belly, and bushy gray mustache that covered his lips. I'd never seen him without a toothpick hanging from his mouth and a suspicious scowl on his wrinkled face. He kept his hunting rifle prominently displayed behind the counter to top off the persona that just screamed, "Ya'll don't mess with me; I have guns."

In fact, I think he even wore a button on his overalls that said just that.

"Old Tom is packing enough heat to take on a small army at that worn-down feed store of his," Laurie told Evie. "No doubt about that."

Evie swallowed hard, her eyes wide as saucers. I could almost see the gears turning in her head as she tried to determine whether we were pulling her leg.

"Anyway! Back to Laurie's idea. I think it's brilliant," Josephine said. She gestured enthusiastically with her spoon. "The cat could lead us right to critical evidence. She might even know precisely what paperwork contains information we should check into."

I raised my eyebrow. "The cat that didn't know what a Thursday was?" Visions of the chaos unleashed last time Belladonna snuck out with Nugget flickered through my thoughts. "It just seems risky. How are we supposed to talk to the cat on the glowing, flashing platter with Mabel in the store?"

"We'll explain to the cats they need to wait until she's taking trash to the dumpster, or we tell them to talk to us," Laurie pointed out reasonably.

"Are you kidding me? You think they'll—"

Josephine waved off my concern. "A minor hiccup. The benefits outweigh any potential risks, and it's better to have them all there in case we need it than be there and need it and not have it." She turned an entreating gaze on me. "Surely you can see that."

I still hesitated, worry gnawing at my conscience. Evie had been conspicuously silent, and we exchanged uneasy glances. Finally, my daughter spoke up.

"I don't know, you guys." Evie bit her lip. "Maybe Mom's right about this. We got lucky last time that Belladonna led us somewhere useful. But bringing them into the actual crime scene?" She shook her head doubtfully.

"Where's your sense of adventure, dear?" Josephine asked. "Fortune favors the bold, you know."

"We're trying to solve a murder, not go skydiving," I pointed out wryly. "Dragging that plate outside of the shelter is just incredibly risky."

Laurie leaned forward, expression earnest. "I get your worries, believe me. But you're right. This is a possible murder, and Nugget is the only person we're a hundred percent sure isn't lying to us."

"There's no telling what secrets Harold hid in plain sight that only Nugget would recognize the significance of," Josephine added eagerly. "He clearly trusted that cat."

Suddenly, everyone was an expert on cats, the platter, and Nugget.

My gut still recoiled at the idea of dragging the plate into the crime scene or Nugget into the thick of things again. But Laurie and Josephine both made compelling arguments...

Evie chewed her lip, looking troubled, but finally sighed.

"I really don't like it," she admitted. "It feels risky and kind of unfair to Nugget, honestly. But..." She met my gaze. "They have a point that the cat knows things we don't. About that space and the people in it. She could find the stuff we'd overlook."

I scrubbed a hand over my face, torn.

I understood their reasoning—with Nugget physically present, we'd have instant access to her knowledge versus trying to extract and interpret it secondhand later. And her unique perspective might allow her to identify clues we'd miss...

Still, my impulse was to protect the vulnerable creature, not subject her to further distress.

I exhaled slowly. "All right," I acquiesced at last. "We'll bring Nugget and the plate along—but only if she wants to go, and we'll only bring the plate if she wants us to bring the plate."

Josephine frowned. "Why wouldn't she?"

"I don't know. But part of being able to talk to them means we must respect that they are sentient beings with their own thoughts, opinions, and autonomy. Well," I said, sighing, "an autonomy within reason. At the first sign of distress, she's out of there." I glanced around the table. "Deal?"

Eager nods answered me.

"You won't regret this," Josephine said.

"She hasn't agreed to help," I pointed out.

"She will," she responded under her breath.

Privately, my own intuition remained less certain.

Laurie reached over and squeezed my hand as if sensing my lingering doubts. "We'll be extra vigilant with her," she said softly. "At the first hint of trouble, Nugget's out of there and back to the safety of the shelter. And if she says she doesn't want to go, she doesn't go."

I managed a weak smile in return. "I know. And you all made valid points about the advantages." I straightened my spine, resolute. "We just need to be extra careful tomorrow if we bring her. Extra extra careful if the plate comes, too."

"Always so nervous, Ellie. Where's your sense of adventure?" Her eyes gleamed. "Someday, you'll look back and thank us for goading you into this brilliant plan."

Privately, I suspected any future thanks would be Josephine congratulating herself, not me thanking her.

But I held my tongue and nodded.

Tomorrow, we would find out if our impromptu pie party yielded valuable intel, closure for the Goldfinch family or simply more confusion. But tonight, we would enjoy the sweet fruits of collaboration between friends.

The rest, I had to trust, would unfold as it was meant to.

Chapter Sixteen

After a quick breakfast the next morning, I packed up our pie offerings and the cleaning supplies while Evie gently coaxed an uncertain Nugget into her carrier.

"There's my good girl," Evie crooned as the calico stepped delicately inside. "We'll take good care of you today, I promise."

Nugget chirped softly in reply, golden eyes round. I hoped bringing her along didn't cause undue stress, but her perspective might prove important, and she had chosen to come. We'd simply have to remain vigilant for any signs of distress.

Soon Laurie arrived, followed shortly by Josephine, who swept in wielding a bouquet of cheerful sunflowers.

"Shall we?" she said briskly, striding for the door.

I shot Evie a wry smile as we hurried after Josephine. "Here goes nothing."

The drive to Goldfinch Coins was short, and we pulled into the lot after just a few minutes. My pulse spiked as we approached the shop door with our peace offerings in hand.

What awaited us inside?

Would Mabel accept our help and open up?

Or see through our ulterior motive and shut down?

Only one way to find out.

I took a bracing breath and pushed the door open.

The shop's interior appeared much the same—dim and stale, with a fine layer of dust coating the once-gleaming cases. At the sound of the chimes announcing our arrival, Mabel jumped up from the couch in Harold's office, blinking owlishly.

"Oh! I wasn't expecting anyone." She trailed off as her gaze passed over us, and she took in the pies and flowers. Surprise flashed across her wan face. "I don't understand. What's all this?"

I pasted on a bright smile. "We just wanted to stop by and see how you were holding up." I held the baked goods aloft. "And, of course, deliver a little pick-me-up."

"Along with our hands—ready and willing to help clean this place up," Laurie added.

Mabel stared, clearly taken aback. "Oh. How thoughtful." She attempted to smooth her rumpled shirt, glancing around self-consciously. "Forgive the mess. I'm afraid I'm not quite myself these days."

"We understand completely, and we're here to help." Josephine breezed up to the counter and plunked down the bouquet with a flourish. "Just a little something to brighten your day."

Mabel's eyes misted behind her glasses. "You're too kind. Truly." She took a shuddering breath, dabbing at her eyes with her ever-present tissue. "I apologize. It seems I'm always on the verge of tears lately."

I thought of how callously we planned to use her for information, and I felt like an absolute heel.

"We understand," Laurie said gently. "Losing someone so suddenly is such a shock. And people don't realize it, but we spend more time with our coworkers than our families. Harold was a big part of your life."

Mabel nodded, sniffling. "I still can hardly believe he's gone. The shop feels so empty and strange without him."

I stepped forward, pie pans extended. "Nothing gives comfort like something freshly baked from the oven. And like Laurie said, we're happy to stay awhile and help you tidy up the shop." I nodded meaningfully around at the disorder. "We know it can't be easy managing everything solo right now."

Mabel regarded us for a long moment, clearly debating.

I held my breath, worried she'd see through our offer and send us packing.

Finally, she sighed, a glimmer of gratitude breaking through her melancholy.

"That's very kind of you all. I won't turn down extra hands or homemade pie right now." She attempted a tremulous smile. "Come back to the break room, and I'll put on a pot of coffee."

I let out a silent breath of relief as we followed Mabel to the cramped break room, and she busied herself with coffee preparations. Our first hurdle was cleared. Now we just needed to get her chatting—and keep alert for any papers of interest.

"Did Harold's brother Anton come back again after that awful scene?" Laurie asked, settling into one of the worn chairs with all the casual air of gossiping over morning mimosas.

Mabel tensed slightly. "No. Though I've no doubt, he'll turn up again soon enough." She kept her back turned, fiddling unnecessarily with coffee mugs. "That man doesn't understand the meaning of boundaries. He didn't when Harold was alive, and he certainly doesn't now."

I leaned against the desk, pie slices at the ready. "From what we saw, Anton does seem rather... intense."

"That's one way to put it," was all she said.

I slid a paper plate toward her. "Here, have some pie while the coffee brews."

Mabel turned, blinking down at the pastry before her. "Apple pie. Did you know it was Harold's favorite?" She attempted a wobbly smile. "Thank you. Truly."

I met Josephine's gaze and subtly tilted toward the display room. She gave an almost imperceptible nod and drifted back toward the front of the shop, browsing the displays with keen interest.

Laurie stood, feigning a stretch. "Well, I'm going to start cleaning the display cases. With the four of us working on everything, we should have this place sparkling in no time."

As she slipped out after Josephine, I focused on Mabel. "You just sit, relax, and eat your pie. We made plenty to go around, and we can handle the cleaning."

Mabel glanced down at the pie I had placed before her and picked up her fork with a slightly trembling hand. "It looks wonderful. My mother always made me apple pie for breakfast when I was a child. This reminds me of home and Mama. Mama passed a few years ago," she murmured. Gazing at the treat, she began to eat with focused intensity, as if this sweet indulgence could fill the void left by all she had lost.

Dear Lord, if this poor, tragic woman didn't have bad luck, she might have no luck at all.

I sympathized with Mabel's ongoing troubles, even as suspicion nagged me. Could someone with such perpetual misfortune be capable of cold-blooded murder, or was she merely an unlucky bystander caught up in events beyond her control?

I sighed, second-guessing my assumptions yet again.

However fragile and downtrodden Mabel appeared, I couldn't afford to dismiss her as a suspect based on pity alone. Too many questions still surrounded Harold's loyal assistant.

Evie glanced at me.

I cleared my throat. "We can't imagine how difficult

this transition is for you. You must feel Harold's absence profoundly after so many years together."

Mabel's eyes welled again behind her glasses. "It's been dreadful. I can hardly stand the silence without him rattling on about coins and investments." She sniffled into another tissue, shaking her head. "We didn't always see eye to eye, but he was a good man."

I waited, hoping she might elaborate.

But nope.

Mabel just gazed sadly into her coffee mug, lost in memories. This woman was so depressed and folded within herself that she never noticed we'd brought a cat carrier. She never asked about the large bag Evie clutched like she was afraid it would fly away.

Again, I asked myself how on earth Mabel Berry could be a murderer.

And again, I reminded myself that a soft-spoken exterior could belie a ruthless core, and the most harmless souls sometimes hid the darkest secrets.

I slowly lifted the cat carrier onto the table.

Mabel's gaze darted down. She gasped, hands flying to her mouth. "Nugget!"

At the sound of her name, two perked ears appeared in the carrier, followed by a curious face. I immediately unlatched the door, and Nugget burst out, ran across the table, and wound happily around Mabel's hands.

Mabel stroked Nugget as tears filled her eyes. "Oh, my sweet girl! I've missed you so." Nugget nuzzled against her, purring loudly. "Thank you for bringing my baby. I've missed her so much."

Nugget purred loudly, nuzzling against Mabel. The reunion couldn't do anything but warm my heart, even as questions churned in my mind.

"We're happy to bring her by to visit."

Mabel glanced up, smiling tremulously. "I can't thank you enough for taking her in. I worried what might happen when I—" She stopped abruptly, paling.

I straightened. Beside me, Evie tensed.

"When you what?" I asked gently.

Mabel focused intently on petting Nugget, refusing to meet my gaze. "It's nothing. I only meant I worried for her well-being after everything that happened. That's all."

I hesitated, debating how to proceed. "Mabel, were you the one that left Nugget with us that morning?"

"Me?" Her head jerked up, eyes widening behind her glasses. "What? No. No."

Evie leaned forward, expression kind. "We're not upset. We just want to understand why, if it was you. Can you tell us what happened?"

Mabel bit her lip, conflict apparent on her face. She seemed to wrestle with indecision before slumping back against the chair in defeat. Nugget crawled into her lap and rubbed her head against the frightened woman.

"You're right. It was me," she admitted softly. A tear

escaped, trailing down her cheek. "I left to get breakfast that morning. I just really wanted a breakfast taco. When I came back, I found Harold, and I panicked. Everything felt wrong, and I didn't know who I could trust."

I slid off my chair and crouched beside her, offering a tissue I'd pulled from my purse. Mabel took it with a trembling hand.

"What made you panic?" I asked gently.

Mabel squeezed her eyes shut as if in pain.

"We want to help, but you must tell us what's happening."

When she opened them again, the words spilled out in a desolate murmur. "I don't think it was an accident. I think Harold was murdered. But I think if I say anything, I might be next."

Beside me, Evie inhaled sharply.

Mabel gazed pleadingly between us. "You have to understand; I had no part in it. But I think... I think I know who did. And I think he knows I know."

"Who?" Evie, Laurie, Josephine, and I all asked in perfect unison, popping up from various places around the break room and doorway like meerkats on alert.

Mabel clutched Nugget like a lifeline. "I'll tell you everything I know. Please, don't let them find out I talked to you."

I met her terrified gaze, resolve steeling within me. "You have our word. We'll do everything possible to keep you safe."

At last, it seemed the walls were crumbling around Harold Goldfinch's untimely demise.

Mabel clearly harbored answers—we just had to keep her talking.

"It started when my paycheck bounced. I wrote a rent check that bounced too, and I had three days to move out. I had nowhere to go, so Harold let me stay here until he could figure out what happened and make it right."

Laurie leaned forward intently. "You said this was a couple of days before he died?"

Mabel nodded. "I realized on Wednesday my check was never paid. Harold was supposed to pay me on Friday. The one before, I mean."

"Why did your check bounce?" Josephine asked.

"The store's bank account had been completely drained. Every last penny gone overnight. Tuesday night, Harold said."

My eyes widened in shock. "What? How is that even possible?"

Mabel shook her head helplessly. "I don't know. Harold was mystified too. He showed me the account on his computer—the balance read zero. But there had been over $200,000 in there just the day before."

"Did the bank say how it happened?" Laurie asked. "Surely they must have contacted Harold when that much money disappeared."

"They said Harold processed a transfer." Mabel twisted a tissue between her fingers anxiously. "But he didn't, and he told them he didn't. Harold was convinced it had to be some kind of bank error, and he kept calling and calling and trying to get them to look into it, but they insisted he transferred the money into another account, and it was an account he transferred into all the time. They even said he did it from the store here."

"His brother pretending to be him?" Josephine asked sharply. "We know he was here before Harold died. Or maybe Anton has signing privileges on the account. Financial institutions don't allow hundreds of thousands of dollars to disappear unless they're reasonably convinced it's supposed to go."

Mabel exhaled shakily. "No one but Harold had signing privileges on that account. The manager kept saying he wished he could help, but their records didn't show any activity that would account for anyone other than Harold transferring the funds."

"What about his lawyer?" I asked. "Don't lawyers usually have power of attorney? I mean, that's what having an attorney is, right?" I looked at Josephine. "Giving an attorney the power to act on your behalf?"

The lawyer nodded. "Giving an attorney power of attorney is entrusting them as your legal representative," she confirmed authoritatively.

"Um, you guys?" Evie asked.

"What about that Monterey Nugget coin thing?"

Beside me, Laurie seemed to follow my train of thought. "Mabel, did you stash the coin on Ellie's property? You don't think whoever wanted that coin could be behind this, do you?" she asked. "To force Harold to turn it over, maybe?"

Evie cleared her throat. "Excuse me. Can I talk?"

"One second, honey. The coin may have something to do with this, Laurie," I said. "Maybe they thought wiping out his reserves would leave him desperate, so he had to sell it? But..." I hesitated, thinking it through, as Evie opened her mouth to speak. Before she could say anything, I continued. "Wouldn't it make more sense to steal the coin first if that's what they were after? Why take the money and leave the valuable artifact behind?" As I was about to ask Mabel again if she had hidden the coin, Evie raised her voice.

"Excuse me, ladies!" my daughter interjected sharply.

We all turned to stare at her, startled out of our conspiratorial bubble.

"Mabel, can you please tell us who killed Harold and why you suspect them?"

"Oh, right," I said to Evie. "Good catch, honey. Sorry about that."

Laurie nodded. "Yes, apologies, Evie. We got a bit carried away there," she admitted.

"I didn't," Josephine said.

Mabel's shoulders slumped. "Anton and Mr. Massey came in right after I found Harold at the store, but I came in the back, and they were in the front. I heard them yelling at each other, and Mr. Massey told Anton to leave and pretend he wasn't in town when it happened so no one suspected him. Anton was really upset. Massey told him if he kept his mouth shut, he'd give him the Nugget coin."

I thought of the mysteriously wiped security footage from the shopping center. "Mabel, would Anton or Mr. Massey have access to the security room?"

She nodded her head, blinking back fresh tears. "Sure. Everyone with a store has a key if we need to look at the footage. There's no security guard here, just the cameras, so we all have access to the room." She pointed. "It's hanging in Harold's office on the wall."

Evie asked, "Did Anton or Harold's lawyer Ross come here that Thursday?"

Mabel paled, clearly hesitant to reveal more. But finally, she gave a faint nod. "Yes. Both of them showed up arguing over the missing funds. Ross insisted Harold file an insurance claim and try to move on. But Anton was nearly as frantic as Harold, accusing him of plotting with the bank to hide assets."

If Anton had stolen the money, why would he be frantic?

"They were screaming at each other. Ross said it would all be fine, but Anton seemed convinced there was money stashed somewhere that he deserved part of. He said..." Mabel trailed off, looking ill.

"What?" I pressed gently. "What did Anton say?"

"He said if Harold didn't give him access to the money he'd promised for the NFTs, there would be consequences."

The words hung in the air like an ominous threat.

Mabel stroked Nugget's back absently as she spoke, seeming to draw comfort from the cat's presence. "That Thursday was the worst. Harold came back from the bank furious. He said he'd been betrayed, and it had been going on for years. When I asked him what he meant, he said it was better I didn't know what was happening, at least until he decided what to do."

"So, Mabel, are you saying you think they both killed him?" Josephine asked.

She took a shuddering breath. "I think, maybe? I'd never seen Harold so distraught. Kept saying all his trust had been destroyed in one day and that he'd never felt so betrayed. That had to mean his brother, right? But Mr. Massey had to help his brother because I don't think Anton could access the bank. Right?"

The bell on the shop door jingled brightly just then, and heavy footsteps clomped up to the office doorway. Laurie and Josephine headed toward the front to see who'd arrived, but moments later, I knew.

"Well, well. What do we have here?" Anton Goldfinch's mocking voice boomed out.

Nugget hissed.

Chapter Seventeen

I TENSED, EXCHANGING AN UNEASY LOOK WITH Mabel. This confrontation could get ugly faster than a clash between feuding cat clans, and we both seemed to know it.

Heck, even the cat seemed to know it.

Anton stepped into the cramped break room, arms crossed over his chest as he glared down at us like an angry bear staring at campers hoarding marshmallows. "What's going on? Some impromptu gathering to talk about my brother, and no one bothered to invite me?"

Mabel lifted her chin. "You weren't invited because you have no business here, Anton. This shop has nothing to do with you."

Anton barked out a harsh laugh. "I'm sorry, but aren't you the shop girl? You're just an employee. Harold was my brother. Everything that was my brother's is now my concern." He leaned down, bracing his hands on the table. "I'm getting sick of you redneck yokels acting like you know everything."

Redneck yokels?

Mabel looked utterly unimpressed with Anton's insults.

I kept my tone placating, hoping to avoid the shouting match I could see brewing. "Mr. Goldfinch, we understand you're grieving and want answers, but barging in here and bullying people won't help anything."

"Oh, it'll help me plenty," Anton snarled, shooting me a withering glare that could curdle milk before whipping back to Mabel. "I asked you a question. Why are all you women hanging out in my brother's closed coin shop on a Wednesday morning less than a week after he died here?"

I half expected him to finish with a foot stomp like an irate toddler denied a cookie.

"Mr. Goldfinch, the four of us arrived here this morning with pie, flowers, and cleaning supplies to help Mabel get the shop back into ship shape so it could reopen to the public. If, of course, that's what Blanche intends to do," I said, trying to nail a diplomatic response that wouldn't set Anton off like a powder keg in the small room.

Mabel nodded. "It's true, Anton. Ever since Harold passed, I've been letting the place go, and they just came by to—"

"Lies!" Anton slammed his fist on the desk, making Mabel jump.

"No, pies," Josephine told him from the doorway. "Mr. Goldfinch, lower your voice. The whole town can probably hear you. You don't want the police to take you for another jail visit, do you?"

Anton rounded on her. "You stay out of this! Family affairs don't concern you." He jabbed an accusatory finger at Mabel. "She's hiding something. I know it."

"What are you talking about?" I kept my tone calm and reasonable, trying to defuse Anton's rage like a bomb squad expert. "What exactly do you think Mabel is hiding here?"

"You know she probably killed my brother!" Anton said as if this should be patently obvious to everyone.

"I would never!"

"Oh, yeah? You were the only one at the store with him constantly," Anton accused, advancing closer and jabbing his finger toward her again. "You probably got sick of Harold chewing your ear off about coin collecting while he paid you pennies and smothered him with a sack of dimes when you snapped!"

We stared at the poker player, blinking in unison like a set of startled owls.

There was a murder weapon no one had thought of yet.

Did Anton truly think mousy Mabel was capable of murdering his brother in cold blood over coin collecting ramblings? Or was he just desperately flinging wild theories around to cast suspicion off himself?

Mabel twisted her hands in Nugget's fur anxiously. "Harold Goldfinch taught me everything he knew about coin collecting. I worked for him most of my adult life. I would never do anything to hurt him, you goon!"

"Lies!" Anton slammed his fist again, rattling the mugs on the table. "Who else could have killed him? You were the only one in the store!"

"You probably killed him because he found out you stole all his money!"

Anton stared at her. "What are you talking about? My brother didn't cough up so much as a dime for the NFT project we were going to do! I'm out almost everything I put into it!"

Evie, Josephine, Laurie, and I silently watched the escalating fight between Anton and Mabel like spectators at a heated tennis match. Our heads swiveled back and forth as accusations volleyed between the shouting suspects.

"You did it!"

"No, you did it!"

"Liar!"

"Murderer!"

I shot a baffled look at Josephine. "As entertaining as this is, it isn't getting us anywhere. Much more of this, and I'll have a migraine."

"Well, that's not entirely true," Josephine responded.

"What's not?"

"That it's not getting us anywhere. Either they're both Oscar-worthy dramatic actors or neither of them killed Harold. This screaming match is too public, too witnessed, and too loud."

She had a point—this overblown dueling outrage they flung at one another seemed too genuine and too loud. One would think guilty killers would lay low—not scream accusations.

"Huh. That's a really good point," I conceded.

"I've been known to make them." She walked away from the doorway and disappeared from view.

"I don't have his laptop!" Mabel exclaimed, still fighting with Anton as I returned my attention to their ongoing argument. "I told you! Mr. Massey collected all of Harold's personal electronics and the paperwork on his desk after the accident."

I straightened and raised an eyebrow.

What an awfully helpful lawyer, sweeping in to tidy up potential evidence and loose ends on behalf of his departed client.

Perhaps too helpful, in my (suspicious) opinion.

Josephine reappeared in the doorway and pushed further into the break room, picking her way toward the coffee maker. "Don't mind me. Carry on with your bickering," she said as she squeezed in next to the counter. While filling her cup, she tapped the top of the coffee maker almost... almost like she was patting a dog.

When she turned from the counter, I could see it—

the tiny listening device she'd left in Harold's office was now perched atop the machine.

My eyebrow raised, but Josephine shot me a subtle shake of her head.

"I'll go back in the shop and leave you two to sort this out." With a thin smile, she pushed toward the door, device planted. "It's a little snug in here."

I hid my surprise behind a sip of coffee.

Oblivious to the break room's cramped quarters, Mabel's frustrated answers, or his audience of close-quarter witnesses, Anton's voice reverberated painfully in the tiny space. I was certain dogs for miles around were howling in distress.

"I don't believe that you don't have the laptop! You expect me to think my brother didn't leave his precious coin files with his loyal little stooge?" He sneered derisively. "Massey doesn't have anything!"

He seemed too sure of that.

"I am not his stooge! I don't have his blasted laptop or any files related to the NFT project. I have only my own outdated computer." Mabel gestured sharply in the general direction of the office next to the break room as if we could all see the computer through the wall. "You want to look in it? Go look!"

Nugget hissed.

"I don't believe a word out of your lying mouth.

You're hiding something. I know you're hiding something. And if I find out you've been playing me for a fool, I'll do exactly what you did to my brother. You hear me?"

Nugget hissed again and flexed her claws.

I shot to my feet. "Okay, that's quite enough, young man!" I squeezed between the chairs and tried to put myself firmly between Anton and Mabel. "I think it's time you explained exactly where all these accusations and threats are coming from. The police don't believe your brother was murdered, but both of you seem sure someone killed him, and you're both blaming each other." I crossed my arms. "Out with it! Why are you attacking her?"

For an instant, Anton looked ready to bellow more threats.

But after a calculating moment, he seemed to realize he was outnumbered. "Fine! What do I care who knows?" he spat. "You want to know why I think Mabel is behind all this?"

"Yes," Evie said.

"It would help us understand what you're talking about," Laurie added.

"Why don't you sit down?" I asked him.

He threw himself into a chair, glaring around at all of us. I slid back into my seat and nodded encouragingly, hoping he was ready to have a civil conversation instead of just hurling accusations.

"Mabel has been stealing from my brother for years,"

Anton began, jabbing his finger on the table for emphasis. "Skimming a little here, siphoning away there. Harold was too trusting to notice."

"I have not!" Mabel gasped, looking utterly insulted by Anton's accusation. She drew herself up to her full height in the chair, Nugget still on her lap—which was, admittedly, about as intimidating as an offended kitten.

"You did! But last week, Harold finally caught on. He realized that over $200,000 had somehow vanished from the store's accounts overnight. And he knew Mabel had to be behind it."

"You're lying!" she shouted, puffing up in indignation. "I would never do anything like that! And Harold would never say that about me!"

Anton shook his head bitterly. "Oh, no? My brother confronted you about it and told you he knew what you'd been up to. And you want to know what she said?" he asked us. "Mabel told Harold there must have been a computer glitch or something. Just brushed it off and said not to worry, she'd 'take care of it.'"

Mabel was watching Anton intently now, tears running down her face. "That's not what happened," she said slowly. "I didn't say that. I didn't do that. You're lying." She looked down, and Nugget began licking the tears from Mabel's face.

"Look at her! Look how guilty she looks!" Anton slammed his fist on the table again. "And when Harold wouldn't back down and threatened to go to the police, she decided to get rid of him. I know my brother—he wouldn't have let himself be swindled by some mousy shop girl without a fight."

I looked back and forth between the angry Anton and defeated Mabel, wondering if she did what he said. After all, Harold believed...

Wait a minute.

Wait just a minute, here...

Anton never specifically said who he got all this information from.

Did he?

I thought back...

No. He didn't.

He never specifically said Harold told him.

"Mr. Goldfinch," I began gently. "Did your brother Harold actually tell you these things directly? About the missing money and accusations against Mabel?"

Anton's face flushed an even deeper red as he shook his head angrily. "No, of course not. My brother never asked me for help or discussed his personal affairs with me. He was the older brother, the responsible one." He slammed his fist on the table. "But his lawyer, Ross Massey, called me at the beginning of last week in Vegas and told me the NFT project wouldn't be funded because Mabel had stolen all the money!"

"Did he, now?" Josephine asked quietly from the door.

"He did!" Harold's brother jabbed an accusatory finger at her. "According to Massey, she was so jealous Harold was funding my project she lost it and siphoned away all his money out of spite. Been stealing a little here and a little there for years, but this was the last straw."

Mabel's head shot up. "That's a lie!" she cried. "I never stole anything, and I certainly wasn't jealous of Anton's NFT idea." She turned to me pleadingly. "You have to believe me. I would never do that to Harold. He was like family."

Evie reached out and squeezed her hand. "I'm pretty sure we all believe you. Especially considering it's kind of obvious what happened now."

Anton blinked, clearly not expecting her statement. "Wait. What?"

I let out a breath. "Yeah, I think I've got it too."

Josephine raised one elegant eyebrow. "Well, if anyone is still clueless, they're a bit daft at this point," she declared bluntly.

Laurie nodded.

Anton looked around in confusion, clearly still lost. "What are you all on about?" he demanded. "I just laid out clear evidence that she's the thief and murderer!"

I was about to explain to Hurricane Anton why he was wrong when the front door suddenly banged open again, making us all jump.

"Are you expecting anyone else?" I asked Mabel.

"No, but I wasn't expecting any of you."

Fair point, I thought to myself, just as Ross Massey appeared in the break room doorway, sidling up next to Josephine with a sly grin.

"Well, a nice little party we have going on here." His arrogant gaze traveled over our group, but I noticed it lingered slightly longer on Anton. Ross's voice oozed forced casualness, but his sharp eyes cataloged each of us like a tactician sizing up new recruits.

"Mr. Massey," Josephine said, her voice flat and icy as she stared him down. "What an unexpected surprise." She crossed her arms and regarded him coolly, one eyebrow arched in silent challenge.

"I happened to be in the area and thought I'd stop by to check on things." His smile didn't reach his eyes. "But I see you ladies already have that covered."

His oily tone made my skin crawl.

Josephine rose gracefully from her chair. "As you can see, we're simply lending a hand tidying up the shop."

Massey chuckled, though there was no warmth to the sound. "I can see you're enjoying the pie and coffee."

"We brought the pie." Josephine kept her expression smoothly contemptuous while Massey seemed to be gauging how far he could push her. His gaze darted about the break room again, then it stopped on Anton again.

What was the shifty lawyer really doing here?

"I appreciate your concern, Mr. Massey, but as you can see, I have everything well in hand and lots of help."

Mabel nervously glanced toward the front door. "Thank you for stopping by."

But Massey didn't budge.

"You're welcome, but not so fast."

Mabel's eyes darted between Massey and Josephine as the palpable tension mounted. Glancing around at the rest of us, I could see apprehension written clearly across her delicate features.

"I think we should have a little chat first." He pushed farther into the break room, casually picking up magazines and books off the table to examine them. "For instance, I'm curious about what you ladies are doing here."

"We told you," I said.

"You did." He set down a coin catalog and turned to Mabel. "Even though I informed you the shop wouldn't be reopening."

My ears perked up. The shop wasn't reopening?

Mabel flushed. "I haven't heard that from Blanche yet, so until I do, I assume it will. And like I said, they simply offered to help straighten up the office while I catalog inventory." She avoided meeting his shrewd gaze. "I saw no reason to turn down an extra pair of hands."

"Oh, really? Anton offered to help clean, too?"

Massey clearly wasn't convinced, and Mabel seemed to shrink under the weight of the unspoken suspicions hovering ominously over the lawyer.

"You know, Mabel, I don't really believe you," Massey said. "You know why? Because from what I hear, these women have been busy playing detective and sticking their noses where they don't belong."

"I hardly think offering condolences and baked goods qualifies as meddling, Mr. Massey," I said.

"Maybe not." He shrugged, all casual unconcern. "But questioning my clients about private legal matters seems over the line."

"We didn't, and anyway, Mabel isn't your client."

"Anton is."

"Is he?" Josephine asked, jumping in. "You have a signed client agreement and everything? Because if you don't have that, you don't have a client."

Anton, bless his heart, finally looked concerned that he might not be getting the full story from his brother's lawyer, while Massey, on the other hand, looked taken aback, clearly not expecting Josephine to stand up to him.

Massey's smile faded, reappeared, and turned predatory, his lips curling to reveal teeth. "Noble as I'm sure your intentions are, Harold's affairs are no one's business but mine." He emphasized the word "mine" with a sneer. "I'll thank you to remember that."

"You mean his wife's," I corrected.

Massey's eye twitched. "Pardon?"

"They're no one's business but his wife's," I reiterated, holding his gaze steadily. "I'm sure you just misspoke."

At that, his stare turned positively glacial. "You're really nosy for a cat lady." Massey scowled at Josephine, color rising in his cheeks. "And as for you, how I conduct my practice is no concern of yours."

"Did I say anything about your practice? You're jumping to a lot of defensive conclusions." Josephine's smile was sweet as honey, but her eyes glinted. "And your behavior seems particularly defensive for an attorney with nothing to hide."

"Are you implying something specific?" Massey demanded.

Well, we weren't outright accusing him of anything specific.

Yet.

But we probably should have because Anton's story finally snapped all the disjointed pieces into a coherent whole. As I mentally lined up the facts—Massey showing up at the crime scene, securing Anton's release, lying about the will, deceiving Anton about Mabel and Blanche to incite him—his actions painted a damning picture. Combined with his thinly veiled threats to keep us from investigating, it all led to one inevitable conclusion: Ross Massey had killed Harold Goldfinch.

"It was you all along, wasn't it?" I asked. "You killed Harold."

Massey's face contorted with rage, his composure shattered. His guilt was written across his livid expression. "What? Don't be absurd." But panic flashed in his eyes.

"She's right." Josephine's voice rang with certainty.

"It's been you pulling all the strings since Harold's death."

Massey's composure slipped further. "You can't actually think—"

"You did it? We can, and we do. You embezzled from Harold, murdered him when he found out, and staged it as an accident. You were the only one that could have." I took a step toward Massey. "But just in case the police figured out it was murder, you played Anton and Mabel against each other so no one would suspect you. Admit it."

Massey stared at me. It seemed he might confess or try to plead his innocence for a moment. His house of lies had collapsed. He knew the jig was up.

But then his expression clouded over with fury.

"You just couldn't keep your nose out of it, could you?" He pulled a small revolver from inside his jacket in a blur of movement too fast to react to. Before I could gasp, the barrel was leveled directly at my head, mere feet away.

I froze, my heart seizing in my chest.

Josephine turned slowly to look at me, her eyebrows raised in exasperation. "Is this going to be a habit of yours?" she asked, gesturing at the gun. "Two out of three cases, you wind up with a pistol to your head. Next time, we're leaving you home, Ellie."

Trust Josephine to remain unflappably wry even with a deadly weapon pointed at my skull.

"You killed my brother!" Anton shouted.

Massey's smile was cold and malicious, sending a chill down my spine. "Well, congratulations. Now you know my secret," he purred, his voice dripping with contempt. His finger visibly tightened on the trigger, knuckles going white. "Too bad it'll die with you."

Chapter Eighteen

Josephine immediately burst into laughter, the sound ricocheting off the walls as she chuckled with carefree abandon—seemingly unaware we were all captives in the coin store, gun barrel pointed at us by the confessed killer.

I stared at her in shock, certain my friend had lost her mind.

Beside me, Evie and Laurie wore matching expressions of bewilderment mingled with dawning horror. Even Anton seemed baffled, his eyebrows flying upward at escape velocity.

Only Massey looked vaguely amused, the corners of his scowl twitching upward ever so slightly, though confusion still clouded his eyes. "What's so funny?" he demanded, tightening his grip on the gun.

Josephine waved a hand airily. "Oh, I do apologize for my outburst," she said breezily. She tilted her head, regarding our assailant, with an almost pitying look. "Did you honestly believe holding us at gunpoint in public would end successfully? Come now. It was clearly an impulsive, desperate play."

I held my breath, stunned by Josephine's daring manipulation.

Massey's eyes narrowed to slits. "Lady, you've got a pistol aimed at your skull. I'd say that gives me the upper hand here. I'm definitely not stuck."

Josephine continued conversationally, "Sure you are. Here you stand, trapped by your own rash actions." She clucked her tongue. "Not your finest strategic moment."

A tense beat passed.

I held my breath, my senses primed. Josephine's nerves of steel never ceased to amaze me. She had effortlessly turned the tables, backing Ross into a corner with nothing but her words. Now we could only hope he would fold before doing anything more desperate.

Ross's cheek twitched, his grip on the gun tightening until his knuckles blanched. Sweat beaded his brow. The entire room held its breath, poised on the knife's edge.

"You don't know what you're talking about," he said.

"No?" Josephine countered, utterly unperturbed. "Think this through, Ross. You can't take out a roomful of witnesses—knock one guy off a ladder or shoot one unarmed woman; maybe you can spin a self-defense story or an accident. But open fire on an entire friend group in cold blood?" She clicked her tongue, now outright grinning. "There's no way you'll get away with it. In fact, if you do shoot us, you'll make your situation worse. They'll go after you with everything they've got. We'll be national news."

Massey's composure slipped at her words like a foot losing traction on ice. I watched his tongue dart out to lick his lips nervously while his eyes shifted around the room like a trapped rat seeking escape. "Maybe I'm past caring about consequences," he told her. "Maybe I have a plan you know nothing about."

"And maybe you can't count," Anton told him.

Massey looked at him.

"That's a Smith & Wesson Model 638. It only has five shots. You have me, Mabel, Ellie, Evie, Josephine, and Laurie. That's six people. How do you plan on killing six people with five bullets?"

"I didn't need a bullet to kill your brother," Massey told him.

"Why would you throw away everything you've done so far on a murder spree?" Josephine pursed her lips thoughtfully. "Unless... you really do have an escape plan? Perhaps a private jet fueled and waiting at the airport to spirit you away? I honestly didn't think a couple hundred thousand dollars went that far, but good on you for careful planning."

"Don't mock me," Massey spat through gritted teeth. "No one would miss a few nosy busybodies."

"Oh, they might, especially when this group includes the esteemed local vet and the town's cat rescue founder." Josephine affected a sympathetic pout. "All those grieving animal lovers demanding justice, holding candlelight vigils... it would be quite the media circus. Huge pressure on the police. And killing her disabled daughter, too?" Josephine said, glancing at Evie. "What kind of monster shoots a girl with a heart condition?"

Ross's arm began to waver, the muzzle dipping ever so slightly. Josephine didn't move a muscle, eyes glacier-cold and fixed on his.

She cocked her head. "Of course, you could always claim momentary insanity. A murderous breakdown from the stress of having just killed Harold in cold blood days before, the guilt gnawing away—"

"Shut up." With each word, Massey seemed to pale further, his combative facade morphing into anxious agitation.

I glanced at Josephine, awed by her fortitude.

I recognized the steel glinting in my friend's eyes. Her flippancy was an intentional tactic, one she wielded flawlessly to throw Massey off-balance. By refusing to cower or plead, she stripped him of the upper hand, instead seizing control of the confrontation.

"This is your last chance to end this peacefully, Mr. Massey," Josephine said evenly, all humor gone. "Put down the gun before you do something you'll truly regret."

Sweat beaded Massey's brow. For a brief moment, it seemed her appeal resonated. His fingers flexed on the trigger guard, the barrel dipping toward the floor.

But just as quickly, his resolve solidified again.

"Nice try," he sneered. "But I'm not going to prison over Harold's death. He left me no choice."

"What do you mean?" Mabel asked.

"Yes, Ross, I'm desperately curious. Do take a moment and explain to us how you're really the victim in all this," Josephine told him.

"You know what? I may as well. You want to know why I did it?" The lawyer gave a harsh, grating laugh. "Because Harold was a stubborn fool. He refused to see reason."

"If that was a reason to murder someone, Massey, three-quarters of the earth's population would be dead." Josephine's gaze remained fixed on Massey, sharp and assessing. "Fine. I'll bite. See reason about what, precisely?"

Massey leaned against the door frame, some of the fight seeming to go out of him. "The money," he bit out. "Mabel can tell you. He was such a stingy jerk, too stingy. So, over the years, I started taking a small percentage from Harold's accounts. As payment for my services."

"You mean embezzling," Josephine corrected crisply. "You were embezzling."

"I had access to the accounts. Authority to take money from them." Massey shrugged. "But you call it what you want. Harold could afford it. Then last week, I accidentally emptied his entire business account. Meant to transfer just the usual amount, but fat-fingered the transaction."

"Oops," Josephine said.

"Yeah, exactly. It would've been an easy fix—replace the funds before anyone noticed, blame it on a system glitch. But then..." His glare snapped to Mabel. "Then you had to go making a fuss over your lousy paycheck bouncing."

Mabel gasped. "Me? You're blaming me because I noticed all the money you stole from Harold was gone? But I—"

"I wasn't going to steal it! And yes, your whining to Harold caused him to look into the missing money," Massey interrupted angrily. "He went digging and uncovered all my past 'service fees.'" His lip curled in a sneer. "Told me if I didn't return every cent within forty-eight hours, he was going to the police and the bar association."

"But you didn't have it all, did you?" Josephine asked.

Ross's eyes narrowed to slits. "No. No, I didn't."

I leaned forward intently. "So you killed him to keep your secret?"

Massey shook his head. "No! It wasn't meant to happen that way! I tried telling him his lowlife brother must've hacked in and stolen the funds, but Harold didn't believe me—we argued, and he fell. I just wanted him to back off while I figured a way out of this."

"Wait, are you saying it really was an accident?" Evie asked.

Massey's Adam's apple bobbed as he swallowed hard. "Yes. Harold just fell and cracked his skull on the corner of his desk. Yes. It was an accident."

"That you chose to stage as a ladder accident rather than call for help," Josephine pointed out coldly. "That's not an accident. That's manslaughter, at the very least."

"Look, he was dead as soon as he hit the floor. I panicked, all right?" Massey snapped. "I knew no one would believe it was just an accident, not with that much money missing already. So yes, I saw an opportunity, and I took it. If I was going down for this, at least I could try framing that degenerate gambler brother of his and getting out of dodge with what that hard-fisted Scrooge owed me."

Anton stared back, eyes burning. "Lots of folks dislike me, sure," he admitted bluntly. "But everyone knows I'd never actually kill my own brother. I mean, what kind of monster do you take me for?

"Yeah, no, not everybody," Josephine told him.

Evie nodded in agreement. "She's right. I was certain you did it."

"Yeah, Anton, I have to admit I was pretty sure you did it," I added.

"Same here, and I don't even know you," Laurie told him matter-of-factly.

Anton looked insulted.

Ross nodded. "I initially tried pinning it on Anton,

but Harold didn't buy it. We argued, tempers flared. I only meant to shove him, but he fell and hit his head."

Laurie and I glanced at each other. Then I looked back at the gun-wielding lawyer. "I thought you said he just fell?"

Massey glared at me with the intensity of a thousand suns.

"Did he fall, or did you shove him?" I asked.

"What does it matter now? He fell, I shoved him—who cares? He's dead." His lips twisted in a humorless smile. "It might have worked, too. Anton railed around town like a hurricane, ranting and making wild accusations. It couldn't have worked out better if I'd paid him to pretend to be guilty. He even made the widow cry a few times."

I glanced between Massey and Anton uneasily. The poker player looked ready to explode, his face mottled crimson with rage.

"You killed my brother and tried to pin it on me!" Anton shouted. He surged toward the lawyer, hands balled into shaking fists, but Massey whipped the gun around.

"Don't," he warned coldly.

Anton seethed but stayed put—though the poker player's glare spoke volumes, promising unfinished business between the two men.

"I still don't understand who dropped off Nugget and hid the Monterey Nugget coin on our property," I said. "Do you know anything about that, Mr. Massey?"

All eyes turned to the lawyer.

He frowned, looking genuinely bewildered. "The cat? I've no idea. I didn't touch her. What do I care about a cat?"

"It was me." Mabel's voice was barely a whisper. "After I came back and found Harold, I panicked. I was worried about what might happen to Nugget with the place swarming with police, and I knew Anton hated her. With Harold gone, he'd probably fight Blanche for the store." She gently stroked Nugget's back. "I just wanted to get her somewhere safe. I brought her to your shelter, then hid the coin in the woods so no one else would steal it before I figured out what was happening."

Anton looked ready to burst. "You were the one that stole that thing?" he thundered. "And you didn't say anything?"

Mabel shrank back, clutching Nugget like a shield as the cat hissed. "I didn't know what else to do! I was scared and wanted to keep it safe until the truth came out."

"You little—" Anton took a menacing step toward her, fists clenched.

Nugget let out an angry yowl, back arching and fur standing on end. Her claws extended, and her eyes blazed with fury as she hissed menacingly.

"That's enough!" The command rang out sharply. Josephine placed herself between Anton and Mabel, eyes blazing. "Back off this instant, Mr. Goldfinch. We've got bigger problems than a situation that's over and done with already, wouldn't you say? You have the coin, don't you?"

Nugget's tail lashed back and forth like a whip as she spat and swiped a clawed paw through the air.

Anton looked set to argue but finally turned away with a snarling curse.

"Mr. Massey, what is your plan for us here?" Laurie asked pointedly.

"It doesn't matter what his plan is," Josephine said, jerking her head behind her.

As if on queue, Mario Lopez burst into the doorway, gun drawn. His sharp gaze swept the scene, taking in the armed Massey, Anton's simmering rage, and Mabel's tearful distress. "Good morning, everybody. Is there any pie left?" Mario asked cheerfully.

"For you? Always," Josephine said.

"Everybody okay?"

We all nodded and murmured.

Josephine asked Mario, "Did you and Landon get Mr. Massey's fascinating confession?" Massey turned white as the gun in his hand wavered.

"As it happens, Ellie's carpenter friend was parked nearby and managed to overhear the whole exchange thanks to some odd situation with the intercom system," Mario explained with a wink. "Lucky coincidence. For public safety purposes, he recorded the interaction."

I blushed.

Josephine flashed him an innocent smile. "How fortuitous. It sounds like you obtained that recording through entirely legal means, and it can absolutely be used against someone in a court of law. It could prove quite damning as evidence."

Ross's shoulders drooped.

The lawyer knew he was totally trapped.

"I imagine so," Mario agreed, an undercurrent of amusement in his tone. He'd already disarmed Massey and slapped handcuffs on the sullen man's wrists. "Just to get this out of the way: Ross Massey, you are under arrest for the murder of Harold Goldfinch. You have the right to remain silent..."

As Mario recited the Miranda rights, I let out a slow breath.

It was finally over.

Landon appeared in the doorway then, relief washing over his features when he saw us all in one piece. I rushed over to wrap him in a grateful hug.

"That was too close for comfort," I murmured into his shoulder.

Landon squeezed me tight, then drew back to study my face with concerned eyes. "I'm just glad you're okay."

I glanced over to where Mario was leading a handcuffed Massey from the room. Anton still fumed in the corner, but the looming threats had passed.

As the sounds of the patrol car faded into the distance, an air of stunned relief settled over the coin shop. We all stood silently for a long moment, the adrenaline ebbing away.

Finally, I turned to Mabel. "I'm so sorry you got caught up in all this. Are you okay?"

Mabel gave a faint nod, still cradling a purring Nugget in her arms. It was clear the two of them adored one another. "I think so. Just shaken up." She shook her head, looking distressed. "To think Mr. Massey was responsible all along..."

"None of us wanted to believe it either," Laurie said gently. "But at least now, the truth is out."

"Poor Harold." Mabel's voice hitched with a sob. "He didn't deserve this."

I moved to give her thin shoulders a comforting squeeze. "No, he didn't. But Ross Massey will pay for what he did." I offered her a tissue from my purse.

Mabel dabbed at her eyes and attempted a trembling smile. "You're right. And I know Harold would want us to keep our chins up." She stroked Nugget's back absently. "All he cared about was providing a good life for those he loved."

I noticed Anton shift uncomfortably at her words, his jaw tightening. But for once, the blustering man kept silent.

"On that note, maybe we should discuss the estate," Josephine said briskly, turning her sharp gaze on Anton. "Specifically, your absurd claims of promised funds and property. I trust you can put that nonsense to rest now and leave poor Blanche alone?"

"Are you involved in this?" Anton scowled. "Hey, now, my brother owed me money for our business venture. Just because that shyster lawyer killed him doesn't negate Harold's debt to me."

"I think it's clear Blanche will need new representation, yes?" Josephine clicked her tongue. "Assuming that will be me, let's look at the facts, shall we? Your brother's staff had no knowledge of this supposed financing agreement you claimed with Harold. His wife knew nothing of it. You don't have evidence to support this so-called deal."

She took a step toward Anton, eyes flashing. "I think you saw Harold's death as a chance to con his widow out of money and assets. And it's despicable."

Anton bristled, puffing out his broad chest defensively. But under Josephine's relentlessly stern glare, he seemed to deflate. "All right, fine," he bit out. "Harold may have been... slow to commit to investing in the NFT project. But he did agree to fund it eventually!"

At Josephine's pointed look, he amended sullenly, "Or at least consider helping get it started. Look, my cash flow in Vegas hasn't been great lately, okay? I saw an opportunity with Harold's tech skills and connections. Sue me for trying to better my situation."

I suppressed an eye roll at his self-pitying tone.

"Be that as it may, you can't demand what was never agreed to in writing," Josephine told him.

Anton crossed his arms, looking ready to argue further. But finally, he gave a terse nod. "Yeah, whatever." His eyes narrowed, flashing with anger. "I'll talk to her, then. If there's nothing else important, I'll be going." Anton moved toward the door, his steps heavy. "Need to go check on my sister-in-law."

He paused with his hand on the door and glanced back at Mabel with a fierce scowl. "You got lucky, lady. I've still got my doubts about you and that missing money. If I find out you pocketed any of it..."

He trailed off menacingly, and Mabel shrank back.

Finally, Anton turned away with a derisive snort. He shot us all one final glare. "Adios. It's been terrible knowing you."

The door slammed behind him with an air of grim finality.

Josephine clicked her tongue disapprovingly. "What an absolute troll of a man."

"No kidding. Harold did tell Blanche about the NFT thing."

"No paper, no deal," she told me.

I moved to give Mabel's arm a reassuring squeeze. "Don't you worry about him. With Anton gone and Ross facing justice, your troubles are over."

"Mom," Evie whispered. "Her boss got killed, and she might not have a job. Her troubles are not exactly over."

Mabel managed a tremulous smile. "No, Evie, your mother is right." She glanced around the shop, looking small and lost amid the clutter and lingering gloom. "I'm not sure what comes next, but knowing who killed Harold is a huge weight off my shoulders."

"Give Blanche some time to work through what happened to Harold," Laurie offered supportively. "I'm sure she could use your help working through whatever's to be done with this place. You never know. Maybe she'll keep it open."

Mabel's smile strengthened. "Maybe."

With the ugly truth now exposed and Ross Massey in police custody, justice finally seemed within reach for Harold Goldfinch's tragic death. The future felt a little less murky—like storm clouds parting to reveal shafts of light.

Chapter Nineteen

Evie gently placed the glowing talking cat plate back in its cubbyhole in the isolation room. As she did, Belladonna immediately leaped onto it, ears flattened back and yellow eyes flashing with annoyance.

"Where have you imbeciles been all this time?" she demanded imperiously.

Evie looked surprised by the cat's fury. "Bella, we were—"

"And why wasn't I brought along?"

"Brought along? We went to—"

"I specifically understood that I was to be included in this excursion, yet I've been trapped in this room all morning! Alone!"

Evie looked speechless in the face of the cat's fury.

Meanwhile, I tried not to snort.

Trapped?

The cat that somehow phased through the shelter walls?

Laurie stepped forward. Holding the tense stare, Laurie tilted her head and blinked slowly, communicating patience and benevolence in cat. "You're right. We were going to take you. Honestly, it's a good thing we didn't—Massey showed up with a gun, and we didn't even need to use the plate at all—"

"Pah!" Belladonna spat. "And stop with your moronic slow-blinking! Your concerns for my safety are touching, human, but entirely misplaced. I am a brave, daring cat who laughs in the face of danger! Do you think something as trivial as a gun can frighten me? Caution is for timid creatures, not bold—"

"Okay, Belladonna, we get it," I said, unable to keep the exasperation out of my tone as I tried to cut off the cat's lecture.

Evie reached down and gently scratched Belladonna behind her ears. "The good news is, thanks to everyone, we gathered enough evidence to prove that Ross Massey was guilty of Harold's murder."

At this revelation, Belladonna sat back on her haunches, looking mollified by the information (and the scratches.) "I suppose your work is adequate for bumbling amateur humans. At any rate, don't let your human inadequacies discourage you. I trust his demise was suitably dramatic?"

"His demise?" Laurie asked, surprised.

"We didn't kill him, Bella," Landon told the cat.

"But yes, there was plenty of drama," I assured her.

"And he's been hauled off to jail," Laurie added.

"Excellent." Belladonna nodded her approval. "Well then, I shall refrain from shredding your garments in retribution for neglecting to include me. Now, fetch Nugget at once so I may hear the details from her."

Laurie and I looked at one another.

"Here's the thing..." Laurie hesitated, choosing her words carefully. "Nugget seemed happy to be back at the coin shop with Mabel. They share a strong bond, so we thought it best if—"

"You left my friend behind?!" Belladonna hissed, fur spiking as her anger reignited. "How dare you abandon her when I may still have a use for her. Return for her at once!" Belladonna lashed her tail, clearly outraged by our thoughtless actions.

"Bella, the coin shop was her home," I told her. "This ordeal has been distressing for her, and I think it will do her some good to be back at home for a while. She seemed calm and comfortable when we left—and that's despite everything that happened this morning."

Hackles raised, Bella stamped her paws in agitation, clearly unwilling to have her desires dismissed so easily.

"I promise you, Mabel adores her."

Belladonna met my eyes with a defiant stare.

While Massey was getting hauled off, I called Blanche from the coin shop to let her know what was happening. After getting over her shock at Massey's betrayal, she confirmed that she had no problem with

Mabel staying at the store—in fact, I got the sense from her surprise at my question that it never occurred to her that Mabel wouldn't be there taking care of things.

Blanche also agreed that Nugget should stay with her for the moment. "That cat's a real sweetheart, and I just hate that I'm so allergic to her," she said.

Nugget would be up to her ears in treats and belly rubs for a while.

"You've made your point, loud and clear," I assured the regal black cat, risking a gentle stroke down her rigid back.

She tensed but allowed it, her anger quieting to irritated murmurs.

"We can bring Nugget to visit very soon or bring you to visit her," I promised. "But for now, letting her and Mabel support each other feels like the right thing."

Belladonna huffed but seemed resigned to this explanation.

"Okay?" I asked her.

"Oh, very well then. I shall allow it—temporarily. But that simple calico requires my steadying presence and direction. See that we're reunited promptly."

With that imperial command, she leaped gracefully from the platter and sauntered out the door that Evie had obligingly opened for her.

I let out a small sigh of relief at having placated the feline tyrant, at least for now.

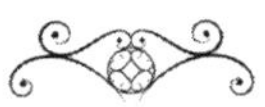

"Coffee?" Josephine asked.

"As long as it's spiked," Laurie answered without missing a beat.

Josephine raised an eyebrow. "You do realize it's still morning, right?"

"Of course," Laurie replied, rubbing her temples. "The early bird gets the murderer, and this bird wants some bourbon in her coffee to calm her rattled nerves."

Landon gently pulled me aside as the others shuffled down the hall in search of caffeine. His warm hand squeezed my shoulder comfortingly, grounding me. Given the morning's harrowing events, I could've used one of Landon's fantastic massages to knead out the knots of tension.

But his furrowed brow told me relaxation would have to wait.

"Hey," he said softly, brushing a stray hair back from my face. "How are you holding up after everything that happened today?"

I offered him a reassuring smile. "I'm fine. Just glad it's over."

Landon's forehead creased with worry. "It was terrible being stuck outside, listening to that lunatic threaten you and Evie and not be able to do anything." He shook his head, jaw tight. "I've never felt so helpless."

I reached up and laid my hand gently along his cheek, feeling the scratch of his stubble under my palm. "I know it couldn't have been easy, but you did exactly the right thing by waiting for Mario and recording it rather than bursting in," I said softly.

Landon's jaw was tight, his eyes clouded with the memory of hearing those chilling threats through Josephine's bug. "Massey might have been unhinged enough to do something drastic if provoked," I continued. "You kept a level head and allowed us to get the evidence we needed without escalating the situation."

Landon sighed heavily and leaned into my palm, the anxiety in his eyes easing. He brought his own hand up to cover mine. "I'm just thankful you're safe. When I heard he had a gun..." Landon trailed off, pain flashing across his features.

"But nothing happened, thanks to you and Josephine." I squeezed his hand, hoping to reassure him. "Everything turned out okay."

In return, Landon managed a faint smile, though his eyes still betrayed lingering fear at what might have been.

"Speaking of Josephine, why didn't you tell me earlier that you were outside?"

He tilted his head, confused. "What are you talking about? Didn't she tell you?" Landon frowned. "She said she would let you know."

At that moment, Josephine breezed up, all nonchalance and breezy confidence. "And I didn't," she declared with a dismissive wave of her hand. "Do you really think they could have pretended not to know you were outside? Heck, once I moved that listening device into view? Your girlfriend saw it, and it was all she could do to not gawk at it like a spotlight."

I put my hands on my hips, frowning. "But—"

Josephine cut me off. "All's well that ends well, wouldn't you say?" she remarked airily with an exaggerated smile.

I held her gaze, not backing down. "You know, this worked out this time, but I'm a little concerned you didn't bother to tell any of us what was going on," I said pointedly. "We shouldn't walk into situations like that without being fully informed."

"Well, if any of you had thought about it, it would have been obvious to you," Josephine replied, as though this subterfuge should have been patently obvious. "It didn't matter to me whether you convincingly feigned ignorance, were aware that Landon was listening in, or were just ignorant of the full plan. Either way, we got the job done."

"You mean you got the job done," Laurie said as she walked up.

"The job got done. What does it matter?"

I shook my head in exasperation. "Josephine, that kind of thing is really something you should mention to us beforehand. We're either all in this together, or we're not."

She waved a dismissive hand once more. "Please, it all worked out swimmingly, and it's not my fault you have a dreadful poker face," she mused, tapping one finger against her chin. "But perhaps you're right, and I should have accounted for that. In the future, I'll consider your feelings just a smidge above and beyond catching a murderer—if that's what you think is best."

With that halfhearted sarcastic concession, she breezed off again down the hall, leaving me rubbing my temples while Landon chuckled and slipped an arm around my shoulders.

"Have you ever noticed that occasionally, Belladonna and Josephine have a similar style of talking?" Laurie remarked, eyes glinting with amusement.

Despite my annoyance at Josephine's sneakiness, I had to laugh.

She wasn't wrong.

She certainly kept things interesting, even if her methods were sometimes questionable.

With friends like these, life was never boring.

Two weeks later, the small Silver Circle Cat Shelter office hummed with enthusiastic chatter, punctuated by purrs and meows from the nearby kitten room. A whiff of lavender from the diffuser mingled with the smell of brewing coffee.

Sunlight streamed in through the windows, giving the worn wooden floors a cheery glow. Our small group —ladies only—gathered around my desk, the office door closed, cradling steaming mugs decorated with paw prints.

"Can you believe Massey actually pleaded guilty?" Laurie shook her head in disbelief. "I thought for sure his highfalutin lawyer from Austin would find some loophole to get him off."

Evie nodded, absently stroking the tabby in her lap. "I know. But I guess that recording his confession made it almost impossible to deny."

"A satisfactory conclusion." Josephine took a dainty sip of her tea, pinky extended. "His arrogance proved to be his downfall in the end."

I settled into the chair beside Evie with a contented sigh. "Well, however he came to it, I'm just glad Ross Massey is serving time for what he did. Harold deserved justice."

"And his poor widow deserves peace of mind after everything she's been through." Laurie shook her head sympathetically.

"How is Blanche holding up these days?" I asked and turned my head toward Josephine.

"Oh, she's doing remarkably well, all things considered," Josephine replied breezily. "Turns out the bulk of their assets were really her assets. Did you know her family was in the oil business? I had no idea, and I make it a point to know everything about everyone in this town. Anyway. Harold's personal savings? Modest by comparison, really. The man lived frugally."

I frowned thoughtfully. "Why did Harold work himself to the bone accumulating wealth if Blanche was already so well-off?"

"Yes, it is rather peculiar," Josephine agreed. "Harold was obsessed with money yet loathe to spend any of it. I suspect Harold's obsessive thrift stemmed from childhood trauma," she mused and lowered her voice. "Blanche told me that his father was a compulsive gambler like Anton—the unstable sort, always chasing get-rich schemes."

"Ah." Understanding dawned as Josephine continued.

"Growing up witnessing the hardships of financial instability must have instilled in Harold a desperate need for security. He worked tirelessly to ensure he could provide for his family in a way his father never achieved."

"You picked all that up in two weeks, did you?" Laurie asked Josephine, her voice dripping with sly sarcasm.

"What can I say? I should've majored in Armchair Psychology instead of Political Science." Josephine took another sip of her coffee before adding quietly, "It was obvious that Harold strove to be the stability he lacked as a boy. He was determined not to end up a failure like his father."

I considered this, moved by this new perspective on the man I'd seen only as oddly frugal and standoffish. His tireless work ethic and protective nature toward Blanche took on poignant meaning in light of Josephine's insight.

"I don't know. Maybe you're onto something," I said

slowly. "Not that it matters now. It also makes his relationship with Anton clearer—the resentment and discord between them interspersed with Anton's attempts at helping him get it together." I felt a new wave of sympathy for the man.

"It does sound like that guy turned out just like their dad." Evie sighed. "And Anton turning out just like their dad must've been salt in the wound for Harold."

"And yet Harold kept bailing him out over the years, wanting to help despite everything. He was a good person."

"Indeed. There was more depth to the stodgy Harold Goldfinch than met the eye." Josephine appeared pleased to have illuminated this glimpse into his psyche.

I hoped wherever Harold was now, he found the peace that eluded him in life. Though justice had been served, I had a lingering sorrow for the turmoil and betrayal he had suffered at the end.

I hoped his spirit had moved on to gentler pastures.

"Oh, that reminds me!" Laurie suddenly sat up straight, her eyes lighting up excitedly. She leaned forward, hand slapping the edge of the desk. "I have news on Nugget and Mabel."

At the mention of the coin shop's faithful employee and her beloved cat, all eyes turned to Laurie attentively.

"Well, don't keep us waiting here," Josephine urged, gesturing impatiently.

"I swung by to check on Mabel earlier this week. She

said Blanche would sign ownership of the shop over to her." Laurie beamed. "Can you believe it?"

"That's wonderful." I grinned, thrilled by this development. Mabel had worked tirelessly at Goldfinch Coins for decades. I think she deserves some security after recent events.

"Wait, so the place is hers now?" Evie's eyes widened. "Like, fully?"

Laurie nodded happily. "Yep. That's what I heard from Mabel."

"When I last spoke to her, Blanche had no interest in keeping it open," Josephine volunteered. "She mentioned Mabel knows the business better than anyone, and Harold cared for her, so it doesn't surprise me if true. Blanche certainly doesn't need it."

"How's our favorite calico doing?" I asked.

"Thriving!" Laurie gushed. "That cat has free rein of the shop once again. Mabel said she lounges on the displays all day like the queen of the castle."

Our laughter filled the office, spirits lifted by the bright spots amid darkness—criminals condemned, innocents and the long suffering rewarded, and a sweet cat basking happily in her rightful home.

For now, contentment reigned in the cozy shelter office. As sunshine streamed in the windows, blanketing us in its hopeful glow, our small group relaxed into the moment, simply enjoying each other's company. The conversation ebbed and flowed, punctuated by fond laughter. No mysteries pressed upon us, and no dangers lurked.

However briefly, camaraderie and justice joined together—for everyone but Belladonna, who plotted her revenge.

But that?

That's a story for another time.

Thank you for reading! I hope you enjoyed the second book in the Silver Circle Cat Rescue Mysteries!

"Fairy Tales, Fruitcake, and Murder" is the next book in the series. Follow Ellie, Evie and the gang as they investigate the murder of the beloved Tablerock librarian Alice Grey!

KEEP UP WITH LEANNE LEEDS

Thanks so much for reading! I hope you liked it! Want to keep up with me?

Visit leanneleeds.com to:

Find all my books...

Sign up for my newsletter...

Like me on Facebook...

Follow me on Twitter...

Follow me on Instagram...

Thanks again for reading!

Leanne Leeds

Find a typo? Let us know!

Typos happen. It's sad, but true.

Though we go over the manuscript multiple times, have editors, have beta readers, and advance readers it's inevitable that determined typos and mistakes sometimes find their way into a published book.

Did you find one? If you did, think about reporting it on leanneleeds.com so we can get it corrected.

Artificial Intelligence Statement

Portions of this book were created with the assistance of AI tools used for editing, proofreading, and refining the text. However, the ideas, storyline, characters, and overall creative vision remain my own original work.

While some aspects of the cover image were generated using AI tools, it was done so under my creative direction and curation.

I want to acknowledge the use of these technologies as part of my creative process, while affirming that the essence of this work comes from my own imagination and effort.

Leanne Leeds

Made in the USA
Middletown, DE
04 April 2024